HAR MEGIDDO

Journey Out Of Armageddon

NEIL S. KRASNER

COPYRIGHTS

DEDICATION

Sylvia Jeanette Langdon Dunst,
who showed me the way.
And Nina Dodig, for being there.

AUTHOR'S NOTES

Har Megiddo *was written in 1976 in Carbondale, Illinois.*

*The novelist, John Gardner, introduced me to the British editor and translator, Michael Glenny, who edited **Har Megiddo**.*

*JanSuzanne Krasner, without her support, **Har Megiddo** would have never seen the light of day.*

CONTENTS

CHAPTER ONE 1

CHAPTER TWO 10

CHAPTER THREE 19

CHAPTER FOUR.. 26

CHAPTER FIVE.. 34

CHAPTER SIX 47

CHAPTER SEVEN 56

CHAPTER EIGHT 72

CHAPTER NINE... 80

CHAPTER TEN... 88

CHAPTER ELEVEN.. 99

CHAPTER TWELVE.. 112

CHAPTER THIRTEEN 120

CHAPTER FOURTEEN 137

CHAPTER FIFTEEN 151

CHAPTER SIXTEEN 165

CHAPTER SEVENTEEN 178

CHAPTER EIGHTEEN 186

EPILOGUE 197

— CHAPTER ONE —

Harry Megiddo was born the day World War Two ended in Europe.

The same day, Allied forces found the charred body of Ernie Levy on top of a mound of hair that touched the heavens. Outside the hospital, the streets of New York were filled with wildly happy people. Germany surrendered! Hitler's dead! Traffic was snarled, strangers were hugging and kissing, dancing in the streets.

His mother could hear wild cries of "joy—"Thank God, it's finally" over!"—just before she pushed what was a little life in her belly out on its own. She had a mystical experience that her baby was floating on a soft, fluffy cloud, a blanket of rainbows tucked under its chin, carried gently in the arms of the wind. She breathed her last breath of life believing that the age-old dream of the Jewish people was coming true out of her womb.

Some thousands of miles away in the Me'ah She'arim quarter of Jerusalem, Yeshaayia Gurevich had gone into a deep coma that morning, and his daughter was worried that death stalked her father. Rachel mistook the peaceful expression on his face to mean that he had already accepted his fate.

Yeshaayia Gurevich was a tall, thin man with a hollow face and a long, bony nose. Never having learned to read or write, he had memorized by heart all six hundred and thirteen of God's Commandments. His neighbors respected him for his gentleness and humility. They accepted him without thought as part of their community, but he was neither on their council of elders nor did anyone seek him out for advice. Yeshaayia was joyous as a seagull but no more significant in his neighbor's or his own eyes.

So, it came as a complete surprise to Rachel that a little later that same day the women of the quarter arrived at her door laden with food.

"We're sorry to hear that your father is dying," they came

1

in chattering and immediately started to move the furniture.

"But...he has lived a full and happy life," another added. "I've never seen Yeshaayia without a smile on his face."

"That's right! I never have."

"Never once," they all agreed, silently thinking to themselves, 'What was there to be happy about?'

Rachel was annoyed that they barged in and took over without so much as her pardon. She felt she was being pushed aside. A stranger in her own home. She meekly told them that her father wasn't dead yet, and it was a sin for them to be acting as if he was.

The women politely nodded and said they understood her grief. They led her over to the sofa and gently eased her down, telling her patronizingly not to worry and to leave everything to them.

They cleared a table in the living room and piled it high with cheeses and breads, salted fish, and plenty of wine to drown the sorrows.

Rachel stared blankly into her father's room. He did not seem to be conscious of the beehive of activity. His eyes were wide, the same peaceful expression invading his face. A few minutes later, the elders of the quarter arrived.

"I've made all the arrangements," Rabbi Tzadikovich, faith flowing without stint, consoled the daughter. "The whole congregation will be here to pay their last respects to your father."

The doctor was quick on the Rabbi's heels. "I'm sorry there's nothing more I can do for Yeshaayia. I've done all that is in my power." "It's in the Lord's hands," added the Rabbi.

"His will will be done."

"Amen..." repeated the other wise men, silently following after the Rabbi into Yeshaayia's room.

No sooner had the door shut behind them than the others in the congregation arrived as the Rabbi had promised - Neturei Karta's, the Guardians of the City. One after another, they paid their respects to Rachel, but their eyes were riveted to the table piled high with delicacies.

Rachel understood what the others were feeling. Most had hardly eaten a bite all day. They tried not staring at the food, but it was beyond the will-power of mere mortals.

Tick tock…Tick tock…came from a song sadly sung by grandfather clock discarded earlier in the closet by the women.

Angry voices could be heard coming from Yeshaayia's room. The guests were sullen. What little talking there was went on in whispers.

Even Rachel's stomach grumbled a little, and when she thought no one was watching, she stole a glance at the food. Then she felt guilty for being so heartless while her father lay so near death.

"Whatcha gonna do?" The Guardians of Jerusalem caught her staring.

"Whatcha gonna do?" They pressured her with a look. Excited waves of stomach cramps thundered in her ears.

"What am I going to do?" She anguished between running out of the apartment and running into her father's room.

So loud was her anguish that she did not hear the Rabbi calling. Sweat beads poured from his hairline.

"Rachel!" He had a pained expression on his face. "Will you kindly come here for a moment?"

One of the women poked her out of her daydreaming and pointed her attention to the Rabbi. He waved her over, shaking his head despairingly at the congregation.

"Father! Father!" Rachel, thinking the worst, rushed past the Rabbi and into the bedroom. "Father," she buried her head in his shoulder and sobbed. "All your friends are gathered," she tried wooing him. "They're waiting to see you."

His smile broadened; he replied by stroking her hair.

The Rabbi came over and put his hand on her shoulder. "Rachel," he said. "The doctor says the worst has passed. But…?" He stopped to pick his teeth. His enormous neck beet

3

red. "We think that your father has been driven mad by the fever."

"What?" Rachel lifted her head and stared at her father. He smiled. She could not order her thoughts.

"Yeshaayia awoke just after we arrived," Rabbi Tzadikovich, visibly agitated, took hold of her hand and led her over to a corner of the room. "At first we praised the Lord for a miracle. But now, I think he's possessed by a devil! I'm sorry!"

"You're sorry!" Rachel's skin stretched taut. "You're sorry! The devil!" she stuttered.

"The doctor doesn't know what else it could be," said the Rabbi taken aback by Rachel's outburst. "Some things are beyond our comprehension. Your father woke ranting and raving, foaming at the mouth. Uttering such blasphemies! I've warned him for months. Isn't that right?" The Rabbi turned to the others for support.

"It doesn't surprise me," the elder called Magor replied, "that the Lord has cursed your father. The Rabbi warned him. We're all witness to that!"

"Cursed him? Cursed him...?" Rachel's bottled-up feelings blew out and sprayed over the Rabbi. "And you a Rabbi! It's a lie!" she screamed. "It's a lie, a damnable lie!" She begged the other elders to help.

"We're sorry." They shook their heads and turned their eyes away.

"Those who the Lord would destroy, he first drives mad," the Rabbi twisted in his point.

"Why?" she cried. "I've heard you arguing with father before. Why?

"What could he have done now that is so terrible?"

Rabbi Tzadikovich's tiny head, almost disappearing down through his neck, said, "I wouldn't have believed it myself if I hadn't heard it from his own lips."

"All you are witness!" He looked at each one of the elders. His gaze came to a rest on Yeshaayia. "Who will be the next to desert my flock and join those who call themselves good Jews and desecrate the teachings of the Torah?"

"I don't understand." Rachel wiped her nose on the sleeve of her blouse.

"Yeshaayia, your father has joined those Jews who call themselves Zionists!"

"No!" Rachel's hand went to her mouth. "I don't believe it."

"Yes!" Angrily replied the Rabbi. "He has betrayed the faith." He hollered.

He shouted loud enough so those in the other room would hear clearly. "He has concocted some fantastic story that during his illness the Lord came to him and said that on this very morning the Messiah was born. Can you believe that?" he hollered.

"A sin!" murmured the other elders.

"Great sin," added the Rabbi. "A fabrication he made up with his Zionist friends to justify the creation of a Jewish Nation. And you all know very well. I have taught you myself." He angrily ran his words together, barely pausing to catch a breath, cracking his pudgy knuckles.

"I have taught it over and over again that the Torah teaches us that the Messiah will gather the tribes of Judea together under the banner of David. It is not for us mere mortals to do the creating. That is a sin!"

The Rabbi locked his eyes on Yeshaayia, who never ceased smiling.

It only infuriated the Rabbi more. "I have given you every chance, and now I give you one more. Recant!"

Yeshaayia replied by broadening his smile.

"You see! He mocks me! He refuses, the stubborn old devil. From this day forth, we, the congregation of Neturei Karta, will have nothing more to do with Yeshaayia Gurevich. He is no longer one of us. When we see him walking down the street, he, from this day forth, will be no more than a figment of our imaginations."

Rachel searched the elders for compassion; she found none who would side with her.

"And what do you expect from me?" she asked, thinking worriedly about what the women had said earlier about Mordecai hinting around for her hand. There were few enough men of marrying age in the congregation. You let one get loose, and more than likely there won't be any more chances. Old and alone and facing her neighbors. She shivered at her future.

"We expect you to be a good Jew," replied the Rabbi. "Remain with your father till he has regained his strength, but when that time arrives, you must leave his house."

"Leave my father's house!" She couldn't believe what he was asking. "I...I can't," came forth from trembling lips.

"Then there is nothing more I or the others can do here." The Rabbi waved his cohorts out. "No need for you to see us out. I will explain to the others what has taken place."

"Rachel?"

She turned her back.

"I will pray for you, but I hold out no hope for you, girl, other than damnation if you stay here." He turned and followed the other wise men out of the bedroom.

In the living room, he gathered his flock around him solemnly.

"There will be no shiva sat here this day or any other day."

He said that he would explain later at evening services. He told the women to take up the food and drink and bring it over to the Temple. He assured everyone that they would get their fair and equal share right after evening services.

The Rabbi's words choked the congregation. A loud murmur filled the living room, fast disappearing as the congregation filed out of Yeshaayia's apartment. Where there was a crowd a few seconds ago, Rachel peered into a silent, empty room.

6

She thought about Mordecai, who had said not a word to her. She wished he were there for her to lean on.

"Rachel? "... her father called out to her.

"Father," she exclaimed, turning on her heels and hurrying to his side. "You're talking?"

"Of course I am! Are they gone?"

"Yes."

"By the grace of God, we are alone finally. I was afraid when I opened my eyes they would still be here. Are you sure they're not in the other room?"

"I am sure," she replied. She took hold of his hand, which was shaking and trembling, the veins standing out, throbbing. "I'm sorry!" she cried.

"You have no reason to be." Yeshaayia stroked her head. "I'm alright. I feel better than I have in years." He lifted her head and showed her his trembling hand. "A sign of the rage of the Lord!"

"What for?"

"For what man has done to his handiwork!"

"The Rabbi said," Rachel sniffled, "that you are plotting with the Zionists."

"You too, my daughter? You are of the same mind as my former Rabbi? "You do not believe your father, who has never, never once told you a lie. You think me a traitor? No worse, you think your father is mad? Don't you?"

"No, father," she replied, not wanting to upset him further. "I do not think you crazy." She thought simultaneously that after his body had rested, his mind would heal. "Nor do I believe you are plotting with the Zionists. Actually, if you want to know the truth, I do not know what to think. You haven't yet told me your side of the story."

"Then I will tell you," He replied. "And you can decide for yourself whether I'm a Zionist or not."

Rachel was calmed, in spite of herself, by an aura of peace and tranquility radiating from her father.

7

"I am plotting. I admit it, but not with anyone other than the Lord himself. I'm no Zionist! You know that! When would I have had the time to plot without you finding out?"

"That's true…"

"Remember," he continued, "just before I passed out that last time?"

"Yes…"

"I was talking about finding you a husband." She blushed.

"I was saying that that young man Mordecai would be a fine catch."

Rachel shrugged, pretending that she didn't know what her father was talking about. She thought to herself that all the time Mordecai was in their home, he wouldn't meet her eyes, sandwiched between his mother and father, who were making sure he didn't sneak her a look.

They came because they were hungry and knew there is always food served at a shiva.

Yeshaayia saw the pain that the mere mention of Mordecai caused her. "Then, my God!" he exclaimed excitedly, "I was taken by the Lord right out of this world. One moment I was here in bed and the next…

I found myself by the biblical city of Megiddo, and the hand of the Lord was upon me. As I looked, a stormy wind came out of the north, and a great cloud, with brightness around it. And from the midst of it came a likeness of a child, a blanket of rainbows pulled up over its shoulders. I was struck silent, and the spirit of the Lord filled me, saying, 'Before I formed this child in the womb, I knew him; and before I consecrated him, I appointed him prophet to the nations. 'Go!' he said to me. 'Spread the message to all the peoples that I have sent ye my spirit, Har Meggiddo, and he shall lead ye to Armageddon.' Then I said to the Lord, on my hands and knees with a quick wind blowing in my face, that I did not know how to speak, for I was ignorant. But the Lord said to me, 'Do not say that you are ignorant, for you shall go to all to whom I send you, and whatever I command you, you shall speak.'

"He told me not to be afraid, for he was with me to deliver me. 'Yeshaayia…' He said my name. It still rings sweet music in my ears." Yeshaayia's face was aglow. Rachel had to look away, for the light was shining through the window brightly.

Squeezing his eyes tight shut till he saw a white light, Yeshaayia continued. "'Go forth and follow my light,' the Lord commanded."

"Father!"

Rachel was frightened that her father was going to work himself into the grave. "Open your eyes," she stroked his forehead. "I believe you," she said softly in his ear, "without a shadow of doubt." She lied, not wishing to upset him any more than he already was.

"You lie still."

"But only till I regain my strength," he said stubbornly. "Then I must go forth and teach to all those who will listen the new gospel as the Lord commands me to speak."

"Yes, father," patronized Rachel. "You shall go forth as God commanded you, but you shall not go alone."

She did not believe it would come to that. With kindness and care, she thought her father would come around to his senses. She would talk to the Rabbi and she was sure that if her father apologized, the Rabbi would take them both back into the congregation and everything would be the way it was.

— CHAPTER TWO —

Harry Megiddo was brought home from the hospital by his mother's brother and wife, who never believed his mother had ever married. he said she had married a man in the old country, and she had gotten pregnant sometime during their journey to America. he had said that her husband died in steerage on the high seas. She said that her husband's name was Megiddo and she had her brother promise that he would take care of the child, and finally, Uncle Sol swore to his sister that the baby would carry its father's name.

"So be it."

Uncle Sol was superstitious enough not to go back on promises made to a dying woman, even if his wife believed that his sister was a whore and his nephew a bastard.

During his early years, Harry formed an impression of himself that mirrored his aunt's and uncle's. He didn't like himself very much, and thought of himself as homely and clumsy of mind. He thought the other children hated him because he didn't have a real father or mother.

Their parents wouldn't let their children play with Harry because they had their suspicions that he wasn't one hundred percent pure Jewish. No matter how hard he tried to please everyone, it always turned out disastrously.his aunt berated him in the most humiliating ways. She pointed out the other boys in the neighborhood and said over and over again till he could scream;

"Why, why can't you be like other parents' children?"

Harry tried, but the harder he tried to emulate the other boys, the more his differences stood out in the spotlight.

Shame in himself grew more intense with the years. All that time, he never expressed his feelings to anyone. He didn't have any friends; people hurt his feelings; he pretended he didn't care.

He began making things up about himself. Telling stories

that weren't true. He formed a young man out of his fantasies, a creation out of his imagination. Anguishing over loneliness. nobody heard! nobody bothered.

"I swear that someday I'm going to get even," he promised himself. I will! swear to God!"

The sun's rays glare through dark shades. o tree, no grass, no flowers or bushes, but sidewalks and cars heading in all directions.

People staring blankly at each other and all-around things made of cement. A new civic auditorium, a bridge across the river, an island of garbage between. Horns blasting, people yelling, fire hydrants pouring out water, children playing in the puddles, and store after store as far as a sore eye could see.

    ***

Yeshaayia Gurevich preached a vision of Har Megiddo that did not fit God's handiwork. He saw the Messiah tall and lean, with long blond hair that fell to the shoulders, blue eyes, and a smile that showed sparkling white teeth.

Standing under a palm tree sapling, stretching his arms towards the warmth of the sun;

"Oh, what a beautiful day," Yeshaayia exclaimed. thinking he was by himself, he laughed loudly.

"And what are you feeling so chipper about?"

It annoyed Rachel that her father was feeling so good and he was the cause of her own sadness.

Startled! "Rachel, I'm sorry, I didn't hear you coming out of the house. What...? What was that you said?"

"It wasn't important, Father," she replied with a trace of bitterness. She asked if he was going out today.

"I go out every day," he replied. "To teach the words that God puts into my mouth. Why should this day be any different from any other?"

"Maybe because today isn't the Passover," she retorted, annoyed. Why do you do it? I don't understand. You make enemies out of most, at the best; you are a fool to the rest.

11

Please!" she begged, "stay home today."

"I can't, you know that!"

He stepped round her, then stopped and turned around. I do what I must." He left her standing alone.

Rachel stared after him, walking pigeon-footed down the narrow cobblestone street. She had opposing feelings about pitching a battle over Yeshaayia.

On the one side, she felt love for her father; on the other side, the stronger feeling campaigned that the stigma her father brought on himself carried over to his daughter.

There were few enough Jewish men who would take a bride without a dowry, never mind the daughter of a blasphemer. Rachel made up her mind to go see the Rabbi. She didn't have much hope, but she was determined to try.

***

Yeshaayia, faithfully every morning, after the sun came up, could be found in one quarter or another in Jerusalem, ringing a little bell above his head.

"Gather ye," he hollered to all those who would listen. "Our fathers have sinned, and we have borne their iniquities for more than two thousand years. Our inheritance has been turned over to strangers, our homes to aliens, with a yoke around our necks. We are driven hard, we are weary, we have been given no rest." Yeshaayia held out his hand, shaking with rage.

"But the long years of diaspora are over. The Messiah, Har Megiddo, the Lord's Spirit, is at this very moment leading the last of the legions of Jews home to the Promised Land."

"When the Messiah returns, the desert will run over with milk and honey, and the streets will run over in the glory of the Lord. All ye who are sick and tired of this old land! Nothing to it! You can do it! All you need is faith in Har Megiddo."

And faith was all that carried Yeshaayia on.

Day in and day out, he would go out in the rain, in the heat. The children threw stones. He'd come home cut and bleeding. Their parents at first taunted him as a lunatic, but later it was much worse. They ignored him. Each night late after the sun set, he would come home bent over, every bone in his body aching from failure, that damnable smile plastered on his face.

"Did you convert anyone today?" taunted Rachel.

"No…"

"Did you see your messiah?"

"No…"

"And you're still going to go out again in the morning?"

"At first light as always," matter-of-factly he replied.

"Your dinner is on the table," Rachel said angrily, walking quickly past him to her bedroom, slamming the door behind herself.

"Rachel…" He mumbled a plea. It was no use. She had shown her true feelings long ago. She didn't believe and wasn't going to listen. She had taken about as much as she was going to take, and Yeshaayia was sure that she was going to burst at any moment.

"There's nothing I can do. I'm in the Lord's hands."

He fell into an uneasy sleep without eating his dinner and did not hear Rachel leaving the apartment.

***

Rabbi Tzadikovich was another who rose with the sun. His cold stare froze the dewdrops falling off petals of delicate flowers that dared to grow in his yard.

Each and every morning, he too, like Yeshaayia, left his home to preach to all those who would listen that the creation of the nation of Israel desecrated the Torah. He argued that only God's Spirit, the Messiah, could bring the tribes of Judea together as a nation.

"It is so written." He stood on a box on the hill of Zion and shouted. It is not for us mortals to do the creating; that is a sin. We will be punished for what we are doing!"

He, after all, was a Rabbi and therefore commanded a great deal of respect from the people. He drew large audiences

13

wherever he spoke.

"But what about this Har Megiddo that we hear about?" someone out of the crowd shouted. The Prophet Yeshaayia says he's the Messiah."

The Rabbi became furious. He yelled that Yeshaayia was a false prophet, nothing more than a tool in the hands of the Zionists, and together they had woven a clever lie about a Messiah to justify their evil plans.

"Where is this Messiah?" the Rabbi hollered. "Where is he? If he truly be the one, why doesn't he show himself for all to judge?"

Yeshaayia countered when he heard what the Rabbi was saying, that the miracle of Israel was proof enough that the Messiah was alive and working his glory in the Holy Land. He pointed to the changes in the land since he was a boy. Once there used to be nothing, he remembered parched earth, winds screaming over an empty firmament. Not a tree or a shrub stood in the way.

The ancient cities were covered over with sand and few wandering people traversing the land. Now, great cities filled with the Lord's chosen, sown fields, roads, and schools, and, most important, Jewish children were filling the Holy Land. All this and more he pointed to.

"Our cup runneth over. where once we had nothing more than our faith, we now have all this."

He waved his arm round in a great arch. "It's proof enough for me that the Messiah is here with us. In his own good time, he will show his face to us."

But, alas, the sun set, inevitably spreading its dark blanket over land. Yeshaayia walked slowly home, a smile on his face, a pain in the heart. Nobody paid him any attention. The people glided by him as if he was no more than a shadow passing over their minds.

On his way home, he thought of his old congregation and Rabbi Tzadikovich. He had heard alarming rumors that the

Rabbi was leading the Guardians of Jerusalem in an open rebellion against the nation. The Rabbi refused to allow his flock to abide by the laws of the state.

They refused to pay taxes, would not vote, or have a driver's license. Lately, Yeshaayia heard that there was violence during a demonstration against the authorities for allowing businesses to stay open on the Sabbath.

But the vehemence and contempt that Rabbi Tzadikovich held for the government was nothing compared to the hatred he felt towards Yeshaayia. He felt Yeshaayia was a hundred times worse than the others. Yeshaayia was learned, a traitor whom the Rabbi blamed for all the ills that had befallen the Jewish People.

He called for the police to arrest Yeshaayia as a dangerous maniac "Who should not be allowed to roam the streets, free.

"For the sake of the children," he argued.

"He is harmless," the authorities replied. "True, Yeshaayia Gurevich has received some notoriety of late, but no one pays the old fool any attention. "They said they wouldn't stop him from preaching as long as he didn't break any laws.

But that was not good enough for the Rabbi. He was quite willing to go to any length, do anything whatsoever to get the blasphemer who broke ranks with the faithful. He decided to step up his attacks on the sinner. He fueled a fire that, without his help, would have died out.

***

No stars were out that night. With a flashlight in hand, Rabbi Tzadikovich was out in his backyard kicking at the bushes and pulling the flowers out of the earth, mumbling and cursing everything under the heavens. A puff of dust cleared from his eyes. He saw Rachel staring over the fence at him.

"Rabbi," she said uneasily. May I speak to you?"

"I was just spending some energy," he replied, somewhat embarrassed. "Nothing like working in the garden to rest the old

15

mind. Work the body hard, I always say. Give the mind a rest is the beauty of a garden."

Rachel did not understand. "Rabbi, can I speak to you privately?"

"Why yes, of course, child. "He looked around. "There is no one here but you and I."

"Oh Rabbi," she began to cry. I don't know what to do about father! I'm at my wits end. His health has improved, but his mind has gotten worse."

"Why do you come to me?" he replied.

"You were right!"

"I was right!"

"You don't say…"

"He has………"

"No…………!"

"I can't believe that of Yeshaayia. He wasn't telling the truth." To himself, he thought he could barely stand hearing Yeshaayia's name mentioned without throwing up. Everyone knows that your father is slow-witted, but if I wasn't hearing it from your own lips, Rachel, and you his daughter, I wouldn't have believed he was capable of such crimes against man and God!"

The Rabbi paused, stroked his double chin. I don't know what to tell you, child. have already told you what I think you should do."

"Rabbi," Rachel cried, falling to her knees. I don't know what to do. Help me!"

"I have only the same advice I gave you that afternoon long ago. Leave your father's house. And this time, I urge you to stay here with me. Don't go back ever again."

"I don't know. "She shook, tears flowing freely down her cheeks. I'm so mixed up! don't know what to do. Leave, father…?"

"I know it will be difficult," he replied, laying his heavy

hand on her head. "But you asked my advice. warned you that you wouldn't like it any more than the last time."

Rachel hesitated, on her knees, not being able to see over the Rabbi's enormous belly. Her feelings battled, her stomach churned, her head ached, and her body cried for her to ease up.

"You know who came by this morning to see me?" Rabbi Tzadikovich sweetened the kitty.

"No…" Rachel's nose dripped.

"Wipe your nose, child." He handed her a handkerchief. "Mordecai."

At the sound of his name, her heart fluttered.

"He wanted to speak to me about you, Rachel. You know, he's never married."

"I know," she replied. "He wanted to talk to you about me."

"Yes, he says he likes you very much. He says his heart has been broken by you for all women."

She blushed. I know or knew before all this with Father happened, but, of course, I couldn't be sure. We talked about the possibility of Mordecai asking for my hand in marriage. "She lowered her eyes.

"Well, he's troubled over you Rachel. He's worried about you living under your father's roof. He wants to marry you, but you must see he can't while you insist on living there."

"I see…"

"No, you don't," the Rabbi tartly spat. He wants to marry you and make you his wife. He can and will if you're willing to leave your father's house."

"I have no dowry."

"Yes, I've thought of that too. And I have talked the problem over with the other elders of the congregation and they have agreed with me that if you do the right thing, the faithful, as poor as we are, will raise you a nice dowry from among our members."

"But what about Mordecai's family? I thought they…?"

"No problem," the Rabbi stepped in. "I will have a talk with them, heart to heart, on your behalf." Rachel still hesitated.

"Mordecai's a fine man and, as you know probably better than I, you're not getting any younger. You'll not find another man and especially one as fine as Mordecai."

The battle raged, no quarter given, no quarter asked. Rachel finally made up her mind, staring up at the Rabbi, clutching his pants legs, swollen eyed, tear-stained face. She said, "Yes! Yes, I'll do it! I'll leave my father's house this very night."

"You're sure?"

"I'm sure."

"I don't want it ever to be said that you were pressured into this decision."

"It won't be."

"Good, excellent," he exclaimed, rubbing his hands together.

"You won't ever regret your decision." He helped her up on her feet.

"I'll send someone around for your belongings first thing in the morning. You stay here with me till your marriage to Mordecai."

— CHAPTER THREE —

There was no joy in waking in the morning for Harry. Traversing a new day was pure torment for him. Alongside, riding high in his wake, one catastrophe after another splashed him in the face. He had lost count of how many times he had tried to strike out on his own. He remembered with trepidation the first time he broached the subject with his uncle.

"Remember, Harry," Uncle Solly said, "you're my sister's son, like a real son you've been to me. Try and be a good boy and don't do anything your old uncle wouldn't do." He poked Harry in jest but said nothing to sway him from leaving. He slipped him a hundred dollars when Aunt Gracie wasn't watching. He walked with him to the corner and gave him all his best wishes.

Aunt Gracie - he still could hear her shrill voice. "Why, why can't you be like other parents' children and become a doctor, lawyer, or something? Anything? Make something out of yourself that your uncle could be proud of?" He heard her taunts long after he had turned the corner.

Interstate highway and beyond. Harry decided to save his money and hitchhike. He didn't have the faintest idea where he was going, so it didn't make any difference how long it took him to get there.

"It's funny," he thought while waiting for a ride. "I hate home. Still do, but now that I'm leaving, I kinda feel bad. But only a little." He knitted his brow.

Two hours later, his thumb was getting sore. Wouldn't you know it—the first car to pull over was a police car.

Dressed in full battle gear, the officer got out of his squad car and pointed with his nightstick to a sign off to Harry's right.

"Can't you read?" The trooper sauce red over. "There's a law against hitchhiking on the freeways."

Harry hadn't noticed. He shrugged his shoulders harmlessly, but the trooper took his gesture as one of defiance.

"Wise guy! Hey!" He saw what he saw, and nothing would change his mind.

"Me ...?" Harry turned a finger on himself.

"Okay wise guy. You want to be a smart ass. No skin off of me. Have it your own way." He ordered Harry to drop his suitcase and get over to the patrol car and spread 'em.

He did as he was told but not fast enough. The officer kicked his legs, frisked him thoroughly, then forced his arms behind his back till his elbows touched, and cuffed his hands together.

Harry kept his trap shut all the way to police headquarters. The trooper did all the talking, scared him to death. Once there, he was booked on a charge of obstructing traffic. He was allowed one phone call and called his uncle's house, hoping and praying that his aunt wouldn't answer.

"It wasn't my fault! It wasn't!" Harry was on the verge of tears.

"You gonna come and get me?" He was scared that his aunt would finally talk his uncle into washing his hands of him.

Uncle Sol grumbled that he shouldn't come down, but he would. He slammed the phone down. Harry was taken to a cell. He told the jailer that his father was coming to get him out. "I'm very close to my folks, you know."

While waiting in his cell, Harry counted the lines on the floor and the dots on the wall. He worried that his uncle wasn't coming after all. "Aunt Gracie must have put her foot down this time." He worriedly tapped his foot.

The jailer returned and unlocked the cell door. "Okay kid, you're sprung. Pick up your personal effects at the sergeant's desk on the way out." He turned his back and quickly walked out of the cell block with Harry following closely at his heels.

His uncle was there waiting for him. Harry couldn't bring himself to meet his eyes.

The sergeant handed Harry an envelope and told him to check the contents.

He opened his wallet first, and there, to his surprise, he exclaimed, "My money is gone! I've been robbed!"

"That's enough, Harry," snapped Uncle Solly. "No one has stolen your money. For God's sake, you're in a police station."

"But...I..."

"That's enough! Your right, you had!" Uncle Sol was so ashamed of him that he could scream to relieve the pain. "I...I took your money. It was just enough to pay your fine. Now come on, sign the receipt, and come along home without any more fuss."

What choice did he have? He was worse off than when he had started out that same morning. All the way home, his uncle was sullen. The silence cut into Harry like a sharp knife, cruelly twisted in his guts. His uncle breathed unevenly, and he could see his knuckles turn white from gripping the steering wheel too tightly. Harry thought his uncle was thinking it was his neck he was squeezing.

His apprehension over, his aunt's reaction was almost too much for him to bear. She was waiting and sprang as soon as he set foot through the front door.

"How could you?" she shrilled, shaking the chandelier over her head.

Harry wished the chandelier would fall.

Aunt Gracie, beyond herself with anger, grabbed Harry's arm and gave it a vicious pinch. "How could you do such a thing to your uncle after all he has done for you? How could you?" She cried, banging her hand down on her favorite table, which only served to infuriate her more. "What will the neighbors say when they hear that you are a criminal?" Uncle Sol brooded.

Aunt Gracie berated. "Well, I'll tell you one thing I know for sure. You're going to get a job and see what it's like to earn your own bread and butter!" She called him ungrateful, lazy, not like any Jewish boy she knew. She huffed and puffed so hard that Harry had some hope that she was going to have a heart attack.

"I couldn't be so lucky." Harry didn't want to think that way, but that's the way he felt.

"Go to your room," Uncle Sol ordered, "before you upset your aunt with your back talk anymore. We'll talk later about what we're going to do about you."

He shook his head despairingly.

"Can I get you something, dear?" He tried soothing her.

She whimpered, "I'm sorry, Solly, that I never could give you a son of your own. A boy you could have been proud of. God has cursed me, kept me barren." Her words battered Harry, who hid his head under a pillow.

***

Harry was fired from another job, the second time in a year. Telling his aunt was pure hell for him. The same old story—she ranted and raved, "When are you going to grow up? All our neighbor's children are already married. Why can't you be like everybody else?"

As soon as he woke in the morning, Aunt Gracie started right in. She nagged Harry to do his share of the work in the house. He washed dishes, scrubbed floors, he dusted the furniture, and took the garbage out. He polished the good silverware that he had never seen used, he ironed clothes, and blushed when he came across a pair of his aunt's flimsy panties.

That afternoon his aunt gave him a shopping list and sent him to the supermarket. He filled his cart to overflowing, constantly dropping his shopping on the floor.

The checkout lines were long but longer for Harry than the other customers. They kept cutting ahead of him in line, saying that if he didn't mind, they were in a hurry. Harry politely nodded that it was okay for them to go ahead. It wasn't, but he was too timid to say anything else.

Finally, he reached the cash register. His bill was rung up, he paid what he owed. The checkout girl lifted his packages into his arms. "Good luck," she said, friendly-like.

Harry took her wrong. "It's not so funny," he snapped, weaving where he was standing. He wasn't in any mood to take anything from her.

"You're funny."

"I am not! You're not paid to tell jokes to the customers." He turned abruptly and wobbled out of the store.

As soon as he came through the automatic doors, an old man wearing dark glasses stepped in front of him. "Excuse me," Harry fumbled with his groceries which were slowly slipping out of his grasp.

The old man grunted something that he couldn't make out.

"What's that?" The old man held a card under his nose.

"Hold it," said Harry, setting the packages down on the sidewalk. "Okay, okay. Hold your whistle." He took the card and read. "I'm a deaf mute. I make a living by selling colored pencils. Three for a dollar. Would you please buy a set? They come in red, white, and blue in honor of our countries fallen war heroes."

Before Harry could say anything, the mute was shoving the pencils in his face.

"What the heck," said Harry. He reached into his pocket and pulled out a two-dollar bill. As soon as he did, the mute grabbed his two bucks and shoved six pencils in its place. He patted Harry on the back robustly, smiled broadly, showing his rotten teeth. He backed away.

"Watch out!" warned Harry too late. Not looking where he was going, the old mute fell backwards over Harry's groceries.

"God damn it!" he cursed, scraping his knee. Then he realized he spoke and clasped a hand over his mouth.

"What...?" Startled Harry. He held the card up. "You...!" The old man was up on his feet quicker than Harry could react.

Running down the street, waving the two-dollar bill over his head, hooping and hollering. Harry grimaced, felt a fool,

23

tilted his head back, rolled his eyes out of sight. How much is too much? Frustrated, he reached down to pick up his packages. The bag tore, spilling his groceries on the ground. "Oh, no..." he gasped. "What next?" He hurried back into the supermarket to get a couple of new bags. The checker saw him coming and frowned.

"Can I have a couple of bags?" he asked. "Mine broke," he pointed out the door. The checker ignored him and went on helping her other customers. She chatted, taking her time, pretending she didn't see him. "Can I have a couple of bags?"

"Wait your turn," she tartly replied. "Can't you see there are others in line ahead of you? Go to the back of the line and wait your turn."

Feeling awkward, he did as he was told.

The line was longer than before, and as before, he couldn't do anything about the other customers cutting ahead of him. Fifteen minutes later, he made his way to the front. "I'd like two bags, please?"

"How many?"

"Two, I said."

"Two," she repeated, taking her sweet time. "That will be a dime."

He took the bags and gave her the money. Then he turned and left the store. "Oh my God!" he gasped, clenching his fists at his side. "Someone has stolen all my groceries."

He ran to the corner and looked frantically up and down the street.

He saw nothing. "I've been robbed." He hollered and ran back to the front of the supermarket. He searched the parking lot. Nothing!

He went back into the store and found the assistant manager, who asked his employees if they saw anyone pick up Harry's groceries. They replied that they were too busy doing their jobs to have seen anything going on outside the store.

"Sorry!"

The assistant manager was very nice. He offered to call the police.

"Oh no…" Harry sputtered. "There's no need to call them in. You know that one bag of groceries looks like any other. I'm sure that someone made a simple mistake. My loss." He backed his way through the "in" door; it swung open and knocked him to the floor. "Sorry!" Red in the face, he picked himself up and hurried out.

"What… How am I going to explain this to Aunt Gracie?" He worriedly glanced at his wristwatch. It was almost time for his uncle to be getting home from work. Aunt Gracie would be furious.

***

"Stop yelling at me! Please!" Harry pleaded. "I said that I would pay for the groceries. Isn't that enough?"

"What about your uncle's dinner?" Aunt Gracie screamed, piercing his thin skin. "He'll be expecting his dinner on the table when he gets home."

"I told you it wasn't my fault. I'm sorry. What more can I say? I offered to pay. The bags broke. I went inside to get some more, and when I came out, they were gone!"

"And what about dinner? What do you expect me to fix your uncle?"

"I'll go and get some money of my own and go on back to the supermarket. Okay?"

"No, it's not okay," Gracie screeched back. "Get out of my sight." While Harry was hiding in his room, he heard his uncle come home.

Aunt Gracie met him at the door. "What are we going to do about your nephew? That boy isn't a boy anymore. He's a man! When is he going to grow up?" Her whining taunted Harry. He snuck out of the apartment. Her bitching followed after. He couldn't shake it off.

— CHAPTER FOUR —

Uncle Solly pulled a few strings and found Harry a job putting buns in a box, cutting the tips of his fingers on the razor-sharp edges at Fisher's Baking Company. Solly warned that this was his last chance. If he didn't make a go of it, he would have to leave the house.

Harry had been working for a couple of months. He was doing a good job, so good in fact that he caught the eye of his foreman, who talked to his immediate superior and recommended him for a promotion.

Up the ladder to Assistant to the Baker. Harry's day now started at midnight. Blurry-eyed, he was the first to arrive on his shift.

Right off, he turned the ovens on, building the temperature up till the whole room was warm and toasty. Then he set to his primary responsibility, putting the ingredients from the company's secret recipe together, watching it carefully as it rose, waiting for the chief Baker to arrive and make his inspection, one step before the buns were popped into the red-hot ovens.

Oh, how Harry loved to sit by the ovens, smelling the buns baking in the early morning, immersed in the aroma with nothing to do until the bell rang, signaling that the buns were done.

He thought to himself that nowhere else did he feel so comfortable.

He had no more ambition than to become a full-fledged baker and do this for the rest of his life. He came to work today, feeling better than ever. He turned on the ovens and watched the temperature rise. When he was satisfied, he set about making the dough for the buns. He waited and waited for the Chief Baker to show. The minutes ticked by. He was already a half hour late. It was long past time for the buns to be put in the ovens, and still no sign of the baker. He glanced over at the large barrels where the dough was sitting.

"Funny," he thought. "The dough isn't rising as fast as usual." He didn't have the time to finish his thought before the Assistant Production Manager came into the oven room.

"Hey, Megiddo," he said. "The Baker called in sick today. You're in charge. Get 'em rolling."

Harry jumped into his work. This was his big chance to show what he could do on his own. He popped the buns in, sweating. He stepped back and viewed his work. "Perfect!" He shut the oven door, set the timer, and sat down to wait.

In all the months that Harry had been working, it had never happened before, but today he dozed off.

"Hey!" Someone shouted, startled Harry out of his light slumber. Shocked, he jumped to his feet.

His nose twitched. "I smell something burning," he mumbled, still half in a daze.

"Something burning!" He looked back over his shoulder. It was the Assistant Production Manager, running by and opening the oven door. A great ball of smoke billowed out. He coughed and staggered back.

"What the hell did you do?" he shouted at Harry. The smoke cleared away, and they peered inside.

"The dough never rose," said Harry, scared, knowing it was his fault. He was caught sleeping, and he knew he should have double-checked the dough before putting the buns in the oven. "It wasn't my fault," he said, "anyways."

"Oh, it wasn't?" retorted his boss. "Then who the hell was it? You were left in charge. It was your responsibility! Look at this place!"

He was getting madder and madder. "The ovens are ruined. It will take the rest of the night and half the day to clean 'em and get the buns running down the assembly line! You better come to my office," he stammered at Harry and walked furiously out.

***

27

The last couple of weeks had been horrible for Harry. He was afraid to tell his aunt and uncle that he had been fired from another job. He was scared to death that they would keep their word and throw him out on his own. Where would he go?

So, each night he left as usual, saying he was going to work. All night long, he aimlessly walked the streets of New York waiting for eight o'clock to roll around so he could go home. Each week he took money out of his savings and paid a little for his room and board. Anything, just so that his aunt and uncle wouldn't find out - anything, just so he wasn't being yelled at. Engrossed in himself, surrounded by armies of troubles. On the eastern frontier, his stomach grumbled from hunger, but it was too early for him to go home. His mouth was dry, his lips were parched, and his body ached from the tip of his toes to the crown of his head. From the top of his eyes over to the north, he saw someone moving high above on a fire escape running up the side of an apartment building. He stepped back frightened, and, not a second too soon, before a bag of garbage crashed at his feet. He hesitated for a split second, rocking back and forth from heel to toe.

"Oh! Oh!" Then he heard someone running his way. He turned and ran and ran till he thought he was safe.

"Whhh..." He slowed down, took a deep breath, and looked around. Across the street, there weren't any trees, stared Harry. A little grass, he hoped? There was none in sight. He smelled the stench of stale air and sweating bodies. He saw a few winos staggering down the middle of the street. He felt woozy.

"Are you alright?" He felt a hand gently placed on his shoulder.

It was a woman's voice, unmistakably concerned.

"I...I think so?" Harry turned, led by her hand. She was beautiful.

"Are you sure?"

"Sure, I'm sure," he replied, still trembling.

"I'm Mary," she said.

"I'm Harry," he replied, impressed by her boldness. He tottered.

"Hey Harry? Are you positive you're alright?"

"I'm a little out of breath, that's all. A gang of Puerto Ricans was chasing me. I had to fight them off. I lost them a few blocks away from here."

Well, you don't look so good to me. No wonder. You're as white as a ghost, which isn't surprising after what you've been through. Say, tell you what. You seem like a nice man to me, and I don't feel like working anymore. Why don't you come over to my place, and I'll make us both a cup of coffee?

"Jees! You think I should?"

"Why not? I live a few blocks away from here." Mary wouldn't take no for an answer and led him down the street. Harry did not protest.

She lived in a nice brownstone walk-up off a narrow side street. The block was zoned no parking, the garbage was out of sight under the steps, and the hallway was clean and well lit. What the heck. He went in. He was lonely and tired and had no other place to go.

Three locks on the door. She fumbled with her keys. "You can't be too careful these days. There's all kinds of nuts on the loose." She opened the door and stepped aside for him to go in first.

It was lush. Carpets three inches thick under his feet, easy chairs made of leather, pictures of naked women and men coupling on the walls. "Can I fix you a drink?" asked Mary.

"I don't drink," he replied.

She made him a scotch and water anyway. "Come on, Harry. It will help you relax. Hungry?"

"Famished. Haven't had a bite to eat all night."

"Me neither," she replied. "How about me fixing us a little bite to eat?"

"Terrific! Can I help?"

"No." She kicked off her shoes and wiggled her toes. "You sit tight and relax. I'll be back in a jiffy."

A few minutes later, the apartment smelled of food cooking, "Soup's on," Mary called out. "Come and get it, all you hungry cowboys."

"There's only me." Harry came into the kitchen.

"You're enough cowboy for me," she replied. "Sit down and dig in."

Harry couldn't get over how good he felt. Mary was something else. She really knew how to make a man feel comfortable. He thought of himself as a grown man and never had he eaten dinner with a woman.

She kept a nonstop, one-way conversation going, for which Harry was thankful.

"My mother died when I was a little girl. My father was an alcoholic and deserted me when I was sixteen. This big shot in our small town gave me a job working as a maid in his house. The old guy couldn't keep his clammy hands off me, and one day, his old bat of a wife caught us together, so I split and came to the Big Apple looking to find my fame and fortune."

Harry stared around the apartment. "How do you manage it?" he asked.

"You mean all this? It is plush, I must admit."

"How do you do it?"

"Oh, I thought you knew," she replied. "I work that corner that I met you on."

Harry almost fell backwards in his chair. "You mean, you're a......"

"Prostitute," she said it for him without a trace of embarrassment. "Yes, that among other things. I turn a few tricks, sell a little dope. Why not? It's better pay than any other job I could find. And if I wasn't getting paid for lying flat on my back, I would be giving it away for nothing. Why not, I ask you?"

"Don't you want anything better for yourself?"

"Sure," Mary replied. "Doesn't everyone? I'm a member of this group that believes in radical social change. I work hard trying to change things for everybody, not just myself. I'm very politically inclined, you know. I spend all my free time protesting the rich exploiting the poor."

Harry was glad the subject had changed. "You have enough to eat?" she asked.

"More than enough," he replied, patting his swollen stomach. "That was delicious. I'm stuffed." Mary pushed her chair back and began clearing the table. She unexpectedly leaned across the table and kissed Harry lightly on the lips. "

"What was that for?" He blushed.

"Just because," she replied, and told him to go on into the living room while she cleaned up.

In the living room, Harry worried that Mary was going to charge him for her favors. He reached in his pocket and pulled out his wallet. Two dollars. He hoped it was enough.

Time was neither here nor there. It passed quickly in Mary's company. There was no mention of him having to pay for her time. She seemed to genuinely enjoy his company. They talked and drank and listened to music. Mary asked if he would like to dance.

He replied that he didn't know how. He was embarrassed.

"It's okay," Mary said kindly. "You're nice, and that's what counts." She moved over and kissed him passionately on the lips, forcing his mouth open. Her tongue darted in and out, her large breasts pushed into his chest. "Harry." She nibbled on his earlobes. "Pardon me for a few minutes. I want to get into something more comfortable."

She fixed him another drink, very strong and went into the bedroom, closing the door behind her.

His thoughts were muddled. He had more to drink than was good for him. His head was spinning. He felt he was sitting on a cloud. He stared at the pictures on the wall and fantasized about what Mary was changing into or out of. His tool stood up

31

straight, pushing out against his pants. He had never made love to a woman before and would never admit that to anyone. The only naked ladies he had ever seen were in the girlie magazines he stole from the corner newsstand - and his Aunt Gracie naked in the bathroom through the keyhole.

"She sure is taking her sweet time." Harry gulped his drink down in one long swallow. Sexual fantasies came rushing over him. His penis throbbed to be let out in the cool air. His head spun faster, he teetered and tottered. Without thinking about what he was doing, he slipped his hand in his pants and brought his tool out, completely forgetting where he was. He was drunk and thought he was home in bed. He pulled and pulled.

"Surprise!" he heard Mary screaming, shouting him back to reality. There she was standing in the bedroom door, naked except for a sheer negligee. Her face distorted with rage, pulling her wrap round her tight. "You pervert! You dirty little queer! Get out!" She raged. "Get out! thought you were different. Get out before I call the police."

Startled, Harry jumped. He felt his hand. It was all sticky. He tucked his penis back in his pants, pulled up the zipper. It stuck. "I'm sorry." He tried to calm her.

"Get out!" Mary rushed over to the window and screamed, "Rape!"

That did it! Harry jumped a foot in the air, landed, and took off out of the apartment, down the hall, and out on the street. He didn't stop running till he was standing outside his aunt and uncle's place.

***

The President and Attorney General of the United States declared war this morning on bums, radicals, and other criminal elements in our society. The Governor of California called for a bloodbath to settle the crime problem. Two investigative reporters for the Washington Post wrote that the A.F. of C.I.0. purchased a controlling interest in General Motors through their pension funds and would immediately move to settle differences with Woodstock Leonard of the United Auto Workers. The Central Intelligence Agency held a six and a half dollar a plate dinner for American space experts and estimated that Israel had between ten and twenty nuclear weapons available for use.

"Israel's in big trouble," Uncle Solly said.

"We give," replied Aunt Grace. "We gave two hundred dollars in cash this year, planted a dozen trees, and took a vacation in Israel, and you know very well, Sol, that we spent more than we could afford because we felt we had to give."

"I didn't feel I had to," he replied. "I gave because I wanted to, or I wouldn't have given a penny at all. I only wish we could do more."

"We do enough."

"What do you think?" Sol turned to Harry.

"What...? What did you say? I'm sorry, I wasn't paying attention."

"On television," replied his uncle. "They said that Israel has a nuclear capability."

"Oh..."

"Don't you see what that means?" Sol grunted. "Israel has no choice. We cannot physically, financially, or economically go on acquiring more and more tanks and more planes. Before long, there will be a time when everyone will be doing nothing but greasing and oiling tanks. The big one! God have mercy on all of us!" He stuttered and fell back heavily in his chair.

"Now see what you've done," Aunt Gracie shouted at Harry. "If I told you once, I've told you a hundred times not to excite your uncle by talking about Israel!"

33

— CHAPTER FIVE —

Yeshaayia Gurevich had an attention span that lasted for no more than a few minutes. He completely forgot that the Lord had said to preach, not search for the Messiah.

On this fateful morning, Yeshaayia called a stranger for advice in the pursuit of the Messiah. He listened, terrified of the rumor that somewhere in Jerusalem there was a villain who sought his end.

"My God!" he exclaimed. "Why? I never have, never once in all my life, hurt a living soul. Why?"

"You have made enemies," he replied. "There are many within and without our country who wish to see Israel destroyed."

"But why me? What do I have to do with that?"

"Some see you as a symbol."

"Me?"

"They wish to silence you."

"Forever?"

"Forever!"

"Who?"

"I do not know?"

Yeshaayia became frightened that his years might soon be stolen away before he could find Har Megiddo. He quickly pulled himself together, thanked the stranger, and held out his hand. But the stranger shook his head, said that that was all right.

"Not see the Messiah? Not see Har Megiddo? After all these years? After all I've done? After all I've given up?" Yeshaayia stared at the Wailing Wall. "They all think me crazy! Even my daughter. She couldn't stand me and left my house." He cried still after Rachel all these years later.

Yeshaayia would survive, he did decide. He immediately left the city and went out into the desert that had been his home for so long. He sent every visitor away. He sat alone, safe, tucked away to count another day, waiting...! Waiting...! Waiting...! For the Lord's Spirit.

Once or twice a week, he came back into Jerusalem, kept to the shadows, searching every face for that of the Messiah. He rationalized his silence in the face of the Lord's orders, by telling himself that the second law of the Lord was to survive; the first was to believe in him.

"I do... I do...!" Yeshaayia raised his voice to the heavens.

But none can really know. No word or sound comes from that silent stony prophet.

***

Yeshaayia's silence wasn't satisfying to Rabbi Tzadikovich. Didn't fill his needs at all. It wasn't enough that Yeshaayia wasn't preaching his blasphemies any longer. The Rabbi wanted to crush the traitor from his congregation. In humiliating Yeshaayia, the Rabbi believed that he could wipe out the knowledge of Har Megiddo from the minds of the people and strike a blow at the heart of Israel. He believed that he was carrying out the wishes of the Lord. To do that, the Rabbi had to drive Yeshaayia back into the limelight.

Today, the Rabbi was returning from the new part of the city where he had been on Temple business, when out of the corner of his eye he saw someone begging on a street corner, holding out a cup to people passing by. It was Yeshaayia. He took a long look. He was sure it was him. He was dressed in rags, his hair was knotted, uncombed, and dirty of face. His neck was covered with horrible open sores. The Rabbi was sure that his meeting Yeshaayia was fated; he was doing what God wanted.

"He's drunk," the Rabbi muttered to himself. "Dirty sinner, blasphemer," he raged. "The demented old fake!" He would have liked to rush across the street and wring his neck, cut off his breath, and watch him die at his feet.

"Hey, wait one second," he steadied himself. He had an idea. Turning his great bulk around and heading to Mordecai's and Rachel's apartment, he designed and embellished

Yeshaayia's humiliation.

***

Rachel and Mordecai had been married for years. He was a tailor. His shop did a fair-to-middling business. The Rabbi, as a dowry for Rachel, had made the whole congregation solemnly promise that they would bring all their business to Mordecai's shop.

They lived upstairs in a three-room apartment. Their furniture was not the best in the quarter, but it was clean and comfortable. There were rugs on the floors and curtains for the windows. Flowers grew on the windowsill.

Rachel could buy a dress once or twice a year. There was always plenty of meat and cheeses and breads on the table; and every month, they saved enough to put a few shackles away for a rainy day.

The dazzle was tarnished by a gloom that had settled over their lives. God had not seen fit to grace their home with the miracle of a child. Rachel blamed herself and traced the cause to the harshness and cruelty to which she had subjected her father.

Mordecai disagreed. "It isn't the Lord's will at all that we haven't been able to have children." He pointed to the six different times his efforts had germinated a seed in her belly. "We should take our savings and have you see a specialist." But Rachel wouldn't hear of it. "Our doctor is good enough for me. He says that he can find no medical reason for my miscarrying."

She was emphatic. "It's God's way of punishing me."

The Rabbi disagreed with both of them. He argued that the Lord wasn't punishing either Rachel or Mordecai. "It was her father," he said. "The Lord is ending his line here and now. Yeshaayia is the last to carry his family's heritage. It is your fate, daughter. I'm sorry, but the evil must be turned to dust and scattered over the deserts."

When the Rabbi arrived at the home of Mordecai and Rachel, he found them engaged in a heated argument.

"No! Never again," Rachel screamed at Mordecai. "No more. I'll never sleep with you again!"

"No!" he hollered. "I will have my wife next to me at night. It's my right! You're my wife!"

"You know what you're worried about," she cried. "You're worried about where the money's coming from to buy another bed!"

"That's not true!" He was hurt.

"It isn't. Then tell me! When was the last time you made love to me?"

"You're not being fair."

"I'm not being fair? You're not being fair. I have lost a little life inside me six times. I will not go through losing another. I will not! Do you hear me?" Hysterically, she stamped her foot down.

"I do," he replied, red in the neck. "But you're my wife, and your duty to me comes first above all else."

"No!"

"Yes!"

"Enough!" Rabbi Tzadikovich barged in unannounced. "Enough! I could hear you two halfway down the street. Strangers are stopping under your window and mocking you both. If you must constantly be arguing, keep your voices down."

"But...?"

"But nothing, Mordecai. I will have no back talk from you. You're a good businessman, and you should know that this kind of public display does your business no good. You'll be the ruin of yourselves! Making your private life open to every stranger who walks under your window. I'm ashamed of you both. Now if you two have calmed down, tell me what the problem is. Maybe I can help." He smiled at her.

"I'll tell you what the problem is," Rachel, ignoring the Rabbi's warning, hollered. "I'll tell you!" She ran out of the living room before Mordecai could stop her. She came back

37

crying horribly, carrying in her arms a tiny bundle wrapped in a blanket soaked through in blood.

"I lost another baby." She fell on her knees. "Oh God! Why do you curse me so?"

"My child…! My poor child...!" Rabbi Tzadikovich took hold of the bloody bundle. "Here, let me have it." Forcefully but gently, he took it out of her arms and handed the disgusting thing to Mordecai.

"Take it to the doctor," he said. "He'll take care of it till I can find the time to bury it."

"Nooo..." Rachel reached out.

The Rabbi restrained her. "Let it go." He waved his head for Mordecai to leave. Miserable, Rachel sobbed her heart out.

Rabbi Tzadikovich searched his misguided mind for the words to comfort her. "The Lord works in mysterious ways."

"I hate him, I hate him!"

"No, you don't know what you're saying. I know you too well. It's your grief speaking, you're distraught. God knows that and I'm sure he'll take that into consideration when he thinks over what you have said, Rachel." He lifted her head by the chin, squeezing too tightly. It hurt. "You're a good girl, and I know if the Lord asks a favor of you, you would do it."

"And what more would the Lord ask of me? Hasn't he already taken as much as I can give?"

"God gives you a chance to make a wrong into a right."

"He does what?"

"Remember when I said before that God isn't punishing you? That he punishes your father?"

"But I don't believe that! He punishes me for my transgressions, 'Honor thy father'," she said.

"Yes…but not this, all this time… And I can prove it to you. A few minutes ago, I saw your father. And believe me! God's heavy hand pushed him into groveling in the gutter."

"You have……He has?"

"It is true. I saw Yeshaayia with my own eyes. As I stared in disbelief, the Lord whispered in my ear. You know what he said to me, Rachel?"

Rachel sniffled, wiped her nose on the back of her hand.

"The Lord said to me to get right over to the house of Mordecai and his wife Rachel. That's why I came by today. God said that I should tell the daughter of Yeshaayia to go out into the streets and tell the people what her father is. A liar, a fake, a blasphemer, and a drunk. The Lord said that I should tell you, if you do this for him, he will look graciously on your grandest wish. A child! A tiny, beautiful baby!"

"No," she instantly replied.

"A son," he tantalized.

"But to denounce my father in front of the neighbors? I can't!"

"In front of all of Jerusalem!"

"Haven't I done enough to deserve a child? I left my father's house as you said I must. Isn't that enough?"

"You must! It is the Lord's will, Rachel, my child." The Rabbi said sternly. "The congregation of Guardians has been good to you and your husband, considering what your father has done and continues to do in the face of my warnings."

Her shoulders slumped. "I don't know what to do!"

"Rachel, you must decide now! Are you going to do as the Lord commands or not?"

"A son, you said?"

"A son," he replied. "A healthy, bouncing baby boy. You have my word."

Still hesitating, "A boy..."

"Yes, yes...," he stammered, short on patience. "A boy and many more children if you do a good job."

"I'll do it!" Her eyes lit up. "A boy! Imagine that! And many more if I do a good job! Won't Mordecai be surprised?"

"I'm sure he will be," Rabbi Tzadikovich said

patronizingly.

"Oh, Rabbi, I feel a great weight has been lifted from my shoulders."

"Remember"— the Rabbi paused before he left. "I give you the rest of the day and all of tonight to be with your husband, but I expect you up early in the morning doing as you have promised the Lord." He thought she should reply, but all he received was Rachel happily humming some dumb tune to herself.

"Rachel!"

"Yes."

"I expect to see you out in the quarter at first light in the morning."

"Yes, yes." She saw him to the door. "First light in the morning. I won't even eat breakfast. Please, Rabbi, if you see Mordecai, tell him to hurry home, but don't say anything about the good news. I want to tell him myself."

***

Out of the apartment, feeling he had accomplished something, on his way down the stairs, the Rabbi bumped into Mordecai.

He was pale and upset. "Mordecai!" The Rabbi took hold of his arm. "I want to talk to you."

"What about Rachel?" He heaved. "Is she alright?"

"Rachel is fine. Better than ever. I believe the change in her mood during your absence will startle you. Come on, take a walk with me."

Mordecai glanced up at the apartment window. "Are you sure Rachel's okay?" The curtains were drawn.

"Believe me," replied the Rabbi. "I just left her, and I've solved all your problems."

"But what about the baby?"

"That's what I want to speak to you about."

"There's nothing you can say that I already don't know."

Mordecai swallowed. "I did as you said and brought our fetus to the doctors. I washed my hands a dozen times. Look!"

He shoved them under his nose. "The blood won't wash off. There's nothing you can tell me. I'm feeling it all now!"

"No doubt you are." Rabbi Tzadikovich said that it was his job to cleanse hands.

"There's something wrong?" Mordecai scowled. "Rachel? She's done something to hurt herself?"

"Stop that!" he snapped. "What kind of talk is that? If you'll let me get a word in edgewise" - He related to Mordecai what had transpired between him and Rachel.

"No…!" Mordecai couldn't believe what he was hearing. "No! I won't allow you to do that to her! She's bound to find out sooner or later that you're lying. It will break her into little pieces when she does!"

"She'll sleep with you," replied the smiling, caustic Rabbi.

"It will kill her! I'll have nothing to do with it."

"I have no choice," retorted the Rabbi. "What I do is not for myself. I do it for the good of all our people, and you must help."

"She'll despise me!"

"You must do as I say."

"I can't! Anyways, I've already bought her a bed of her own."

"Your livelihood depends on your cooperation."

"Please . . . Anything but this!"

"Rachel won't find out unless you say something stupid."

"Please…?"

"You will, or you're out in the street. No wife, no business, no friends, nothing. You want that?"

"No… But…I…"

"Then, you see the light of the right of my plan. I'll leave you, go so you can go up to your wife. She's prettying herself up for you." Mordecai's complexion went from pale white to putrid green.

"Mordecai, believe in the way of the Lord. You'll see. All will turn out right. You have my word."

"But..."

"No buts," Rabbi Tzadikovich pushed him towards home. "You go upstairs and enjoy the pleasures of marriage. Think of nothing but giving Rachel a good time. And be sure, when she tells you the good news, you pretend to be overjoyed. Go on. She's waiting."

"I wonder if he knows what he asks of me," Mordecai mumbled under his breath, climbing the stairs slowly.

"Oh, Mordecai." Rachel rushed into his arms at the top of the stairs. "You'll never guess what."

"What?" he replied, trying to mask his true feelings. "The Rabbi said that we are going to have a baby."

"No kidding!"

"Yes, isn't it wonderful. He said that if I do as he and the Lord say, you and me - A son! What do you think about that?"

"I... I...think that's great," he shivered. "That's really great."

"You cold?"

"No."

"You don't sound very happy," said Rachel, confused. "I thought this would make you happy. Is something wrong? You didn't have an argument with the Rabbi?"

"No darling, of course not. I'm just overcome, that's all."

"You are happy that I've changed my mind about trying for another child?"

"Of course, darling." He took her in his arms so that she would not see the pain on his face.

"You mean it?"

"Yes, dearest. I mean it. I'm happy if you are." Mordecai kissed her forehead. "I just don't want to see you disappointed again, that's all."

"I won't be. I know it. The Rabbi has promised that if I do all he and God say, God will reward us with not one baby but many children. Oh Mordecai!" She tightly wound her arms around his neck, kicking her feet up in the air. She giggled. "I'm so happy, I could cry! A son! I can hardly believe it after all these years."

"Hardly."

He kept his thoughts to himself: 'There's no turning back now for me. I've let the lie go too far already.'

"A son," Mordecai purred in her ear. "Won't that be fine?"

Rachel pulled back, a gleam in her eye. "If I had a wish. I'd wish… You know." she blushed. "We could go to bed and make love."

Mordecai coughed. "You know you can't! Anyway, I'm not feeling well. I'm kinda beat. I think I'm coming down with a cold or something."

"I'll tell you something," Rachel replied. "If I could, I would." She saw the shock on his face. "I mean it."

"That would be a sin!"

"Under the circumstances, I believe that God would understand."

"Maybe…?" Mordecai mumbled. "There'll be plenty of time later. Let's not argue anymore."

"You're not mad at me? Are you?"

"No, of course not," he replied. "I love you."

***

Rabbi Tzadikovich's small round frame bounced menacingly from side to side as he barreled down the narrow cobble-stone street crowded with people scurrying about their business.

Small shops dotted his way home, filled with customers. Small children broke away from their mothers, small stones got

43

embedded between his chubby toes.

The discomfort between his toes outweighed the indignity of having to bend over in public. The whole street stopped what they were doing to watch. He straightened up slowly, his belly jiggling. He swept a cold stare down the street.

The children ran back and hid behind their mothers' skirts. Customers staring out of shop windows turned their heads away. Pedestrians froze where they stood, and on the fringes of the Rabbi's vision, he saw a group of young upstarts sneaking away, smirking, thinking they could steal away undetected. He made a mental note who they were and swore under his breath that he would deal harshly with them later.

"Rabbi!" shouted Nadab the butcher, who had had enough of this foolishness. "Hey Rabbi? How goes things? You want a knish to nibble on?" He stared at the cowardly faces of his neighbors, coming to rest on the face of a stranger. This was a gentleman none too young anymore, straight-laced and dignified. He gave the stranger a second quick look, then turned his attention back to the Rabbi.

"Haven't the time," replied the Rabbi. He winked. "I won't forget the honor you all pay your Rabbi."

"Huh!" grunted Nadab. He couldn't tell for sure how the Rabbi meant that. The implications could be devastating to his business if he had to find another Rabbi to bless his meat.

Hamish Zahari looked on with ill-concealed curiosity. He had a few hours to waste before his plane was to depart for New York. He was being sent by the government on an urgent mission. His success would amount to the saving of many prominent Jews' lives. His failure... He would rather not think about the consequences of failure.

"These hard feelings between our Rabbi and Yeshaayia have gone on for far too long." Nadab said to the crowd of neighbors outside his shop as soon as the Rabbi turned away.

"And Rabbi Tzadikovich's disposition grows more sour each year passing."

"Bodes ill for the whole quarter," another added. "So goes our Rabbi, so we all go."

"He grows crazy with his hatred for Yeshaayia."

"And for this Har Megiddo, whoever he really is."

"Hmm..." Nadab nodded, distressed. "I see this all blowing up in our faces if we're not careful."

"As if we haven't enough enemies, we must tear ourselves apart from within."

Hamish transferred his gaze, first to the butcher, then to his friends. Then with the same air of deliberation, he began to follow after the Rabbi, examining the harsh teacher.

Rabbi Tzadikovich staggered down the street, and everyone he met, a few he didn't know, he forced them to listen: "Yeshaayia is a blasphemer, a liar, desecrater of the Lord's name and a new twist today: Yeshaayia, I saw him stumbling drunk and begging for pennies to buy a bottle of cheap wine. I saw him myself! I heard him!" He blamed Yeshaayia for the terrorist bombings that had plagued the innocent lately. He said it wasn't the Arabs who were their enemies. It was Yeshaayia Gurevich and his false Messiah, Har Megiddo.

With every step he took towards home, Hamish heard the Rabbi raise the ire of the people against this Har Megiddo. He blamed the government for protecting Yeshaayia. He blamed the Chief Rabbis of Jerusalem for helping him. He blamed everyone and everything in Israel, all except his Arab brothers and the congregation of the Guardians of Jerusalem.

Hamish came closer, as the Rabbi arrived at what Hamish took to be his home. The Rabbi was panting and wheezing for breath. His housekeeper rushed out to meet him.

"Rabbi," she exclaimed. "You've been exerting yourself too much."

"You're right, of course, old friend. But I haven't much time. I feel it in these old bones of mine that if I don't move quickly to destroy Gurevich now, it will be too late for us all."

"But you can't do any good for anyone if you kill

45

yourself."

"That's in the Lord's hands," he replied.

His housekeeper bent her head low so the Rabbi could stroke her hair. He saw Hamish standing close by, who in turn stared straight back into his face with an inquiring expression and without flinching an inch. The strained silence lasted for about a minute before Hamish softened somewhat and, politely, though not without certain severity, turned and headed off for the airport.

— CHAPTER SIX —

Back on the street with hardly any rest, no food in his stomach, his belly sputtered gas. Harry thought of himself as a prisoner behind fortress walls, thirty, forty, fifty, a hundred stories tall, behind a moat called the Hudson, guarded by millions of strangers.

Tonight, he aimlessly kicked a soda pop can down to Times Square, neon lights lighting up the sky, blotting out the stars by their incandescence; his nose pressed flat against an adult bookstore window, Harry stared at the pictures of naked women. He especially liked the women dressed in black. Black panties, black bra, black garter belt, black stockings, black high heels, carrying a long black whip, snapping at the air.

Armies of goosebumps marched in single file down the middle of his back to the crack that split his legs apart.

"Harry! Harry! I can't believe it's you! Where have you been hiding yourself all this time?"

The voice was familiar. Harry turned to see who it was.

Startled, he exclaimed, "Mary! No!" He moaned and started to leave. "Don't go." She blocked his way. "Take it easy. I'm sorry. I don't know what came over me."

He couldn't bring himself to look up at her. Ashamed at what he had done, fidgeting where he stood.

"Come on, Harry," Mary purred. "I said I was sorry. I searched all over for you. Where you been?"

"Around." His mind was closed tight. 'Oh no! Why' he thought to himself, 'did he have to run into her?'

"Around? Around where?"

"Just around."

"It doesn't make any difference, anyways."

She lifted his head by his chin with the tips of her fingers, brushed her body up against his. Softy, "Harry open your eyes and look at me. Come on, you can do it; you want to." She

47

continued to rub her body against Harry's. "That's it, a little bit more. There!" she exclaimed. "You forgive me?"

He twisted his head away, a last-ditch effort against his nature to easily forgive.

"Forgive me," she cooed. "Please," she soothed. "Please, pretty please with a cherry on top."

A faint sparkle gleamed in Harry's eyes.

"You're giving in, Harry. You are! You can't deny it." She threw her arms around his waist and squeezed. "I'm so happy I found you and to prove it to you, I'm going to take the rest of the night off to be with you. Let's go back to my place and get acquainted again." She gave him knowing smile.

Mary didn't give Harry a chance to say no. She took his arm and pulled him away from the pornography shop. "You like girls dressing up for you? If you like and you're a good boy, I'll dress up like those girls in the window." She chippered along until he was once again standing in front of her apartment. She handed him the key.

He hesitated.

"Go on, silly," she urged. "Open the door."

The apartment was as he had remembered and thought of more often than he liked to admit to himself. And on the walls, all those pictures of naked ladies. He felt his blood stir.

"A friend of mine," said Mary, "painted most of them. Manwo Malefe. She just finished that one of me." She sauntered over and stood under a picture, posing the scene painted.

Harry let out his breath slowly. "Who'd you say painted it? That's beautiful."

"Manwo Malefe," replied Mary. "I'm hoping she and her boyfriend Urbo get over in time to meet you. I'd like you to meet them. They're my best friends. They're nuts!"

Mary made some coffee and sat down on the couch next to Harry. "What do you do?" she asked. "Work? Go to college? Bum around?"

"Right now," he replied. "You could say I'm bumming.

I'm on vacation from college. I go to Brown University. You know, that's an Ivy League school in Rhode Island, but I don't think I'm going back. At least for a while. Haven't decided yet what I want to do. I might travel for a while, I've been thinking."

"Know what you mean." Mary fluttered her eyelashes and moved closer. "Sometimes I want to chuck it all in myself."

"You mean you go to college, too?" Harry was surprised.

"Nah… Never went to college, other than the college of hard knocks. But I know what you mean when you say that you haven't figured out what to do with your life. I think about that a whole lot myself. Before I met Manwo, I was confused. Now I got me this good corner to work on. I make a better living than a lot of girls I know. I'm far from rich, but I got enough for my needs."

"Sure is hot," Harry shifted, uneasily.

"Stifling," she replied. "Can't remember it being so hot for so many days in a row. I've noticed my John's unusually uptight lately. I guess it's the heat."

"Mary, why…?" Tongue-tied, he asked.

"Go on, Harry," she replied at ease. "Spill it out. I want to be friends with you."

"Why do you work on that corner? You're a smart girl. I'm sure you could find a better job if you wanted too badly enough."

"When I first came to the big city," she replied, "I tried getting a straight job. Everywhere I went to apply, if I wanted the position, I had to get it lying flat on my back. Then I met Manwo, and she straightened me out on how things work here. 'Why sell the one thing you got going for you for a few pennies?' she explained, 'When you could work less and make a hell of a lot more bucks on the streets selling it to Johns.' "You know a gal in this country is a second-class citizen?

"I guess so."

"You guess so! It's true!" Mary became excited. "The fat cats get rich by milking the little people for all they are worth.

49

The syndicate and the Jews run the government, and the government runs the rest of us for their benefit."

"I don't know," he replied. "I don't give politics much thought. It always seemed to me that was for other people. I have more important and urgent matters on my mind."

"Stick around here for a while and you'll get an earful. I can promise you that among other things." She ran her hand up his leg, stopping just below his crotch.

If time were a thing, Harry would have reached out and made it stand still. He sank into the sofa, resting his head in his hands, and listened to Mary who went on and on, spinning a web that surrounded Harry with affection.

The sun rose over the city's skyline. Harry was worried that his aunt and uncle would be upset if he didn't arrive home at his regular time. He wanted to stay and fretted about leaving. As soon as he decided that he'd better be on his way, there came a knock at the door.

"Hey, hey, hey!" A man, bubbling with excitement, burst into the apartment.

"These are the friends I was telling you about." The stranger picked Mary off the ground. Kissing her on the neck, he spun her around.

"Harry," laughed Mary. "This is Urbo and that beautiful woman carrying all the packages is my best friend in the whole wide world, Manwo Malefe."

"Glad to meet you." Harry held his hand out to Urbo; Urbo let Mary down on the floor.

"I'll shake hands with you once, but only once. I don't like formalities. What did you say your name was?"

"Harry."

"Well, Harry, I'm glad to meet you." Urbo reached into his pocket and pulled out a crumpled cigarette. "You smoke dope, Harry?"

"Sure do," he lied. 'Aunt Gracie would never allow me to smoke,' he thought to himself.

"Well, Harry, this is going to be some of the best pot you ever smoked. Hey, you guys," he shouted to Mary and Manwo. "You want to smoke some Columbo?"

"Sure do," Mary said, taking the cigarette and lighting it.

For the moment, Harry imbibed the casual and friendly atmosphere in which he so fortuitously found himself. He puffed and puffed on the funny cigarette with some reticence, but after watching the others, he imitated them and inhaled deeply, holding the smoke in for as long as he could. It didn't seem difficult, although it did burn his throat a little.

After a few minutes, Mary and Manwo appeared totally relaxed as they slouched their bodies straight out. Harry felt a little light but didn't seem to be affected. He continued to puff, taking more and more in. Maybe this was the extent of it for him, he wondered. Just a little light in the head, or maybe it didn't really affect him at all.

He leaned back and watched Mary get up and walk across the room. "You guys want to hear anything in particular?"

Harry became absorbed in the rhythm of the music all the while puffing away. Unexpectedly, a dizziness overcame him that seemed to strike at the center of his brain. He gasped as if he was suddenly placed on a roller coaster. He gripped the side of the couch to hang on. The room whirled, and the lights were brighter and sharper. He turned towards Mary to make sure she was still there.

"Hi, honey," she said. "You get off?"

All Harry could do was shake his head.

Urbo was talking louder and louder. Harry could barely keep up with what he was saying; he was talking so fast.

"You coming along to the demonstration?" he asked.

"I didn't know that there was one going on." He slurred his words. "Yes," Manwo broke in. "I brought along a few goodies for the party. Hey, Mary. That reminds me, you have anything round that I can put the stuff in? An overnight bag or something nobody will notice?"

"Sure," she replied. "Come into the bedroom, and let's take a look. I'm sure I can rustle something up."

"You coming?" Urbo rolled another reefer.

"I don't even know where you're going."

"We're all going down to the Federal Building. Supposed to be a big turnout. The organizers have been promoting this demonstration for a month now."

"Why?"

"To show our opposition to the fascist Jew government that enslaves the working men and women in this country."

"I don't get it."

"What?" Urbo seemed genuinely surprised. "Why? To fight the Fascists! All power to the people is our motto!" He raised a clenched fist. "Against the Jews and their corporate fronts, against the military establishment, the Congress, and the Supreme Court. To stand by all the oppressed peoples in all the world. The Palestinians, Croatians, Iranians, and the French Canadians. We don't believe in countries or boundaries between people. One world, freedom and equality for all!"

"Today," Manwo came bouncing out of the bedroom, "We demand that the poor people have the power to choose through free elections the next Attorney General and Secretary of Health, Education and Welfare! And if they won't agree to our demands," Manwo hefted the bag she was carrying, "We, the People, will no longer take no for an answer. We will act!"

Urbo, hands on hips, throwing out his chest, head high in the air, sucked in his beer belly. "Are you with us?" he demanded of Harry.

Too much was happening all at the same time for Harry to put it all together. Pressured from the others, he shook his head: "Yes."

Urbo heartily congratulated him by slapping him robustly on the back. "Good! One more comrade patriot added to the ranks."

"Know what time it is?" Manwo asked Mary.

52

"It's early. We still have a few hours before we have to be leaving."

"Let's have a party," Urbo suggested gaily. "A Thanksgiving Party!"

"What is there to be thankful for?" Mary threw a damper on the idea. "The world is sickening, people selling babies by the pound, corporations poisoning the environment, war, hunger. What is there to celebrate? I ask you?"

"A new friend," replied Urbo. "A new comrade in arms armed against the fascists is something to be thankful for."

The music got louder and louder. In spite of himself, Harry found himself warming up to Mary's friends. They talked to him like he was a somebody. That was a novelty. He was having the time of his life.

Harry relaxed enough even to dance a little with Mary who was getting awfully high herself. She brushed and bumped her body up against his, shoved her rear into his crotch.

Turned on, feeling good and loose, Mary guided Harry over to the couch and gently eased him down on his back.

"Now this is the life," he sighed contentedly. "This is how it should be all the time."

"Like me?" Mary leaned over, pecking his face with tickling kisses.

"I like you." She trailed her lips down to his mouth and forced it open with a persistent tongue. Wider and wider, stretching his lips as far apart as possible.

He was running his hand down her back, heading for her pants when Mary lunged forward, gagging! She wretched her lunch all over Harry's face and into his wide-open mouth.

He swallowed once, twice before he choked. He threw her off and staggered to his feet.

Urbo and Manwo stared at him. Urbo cracked a smile and snickered. Manwo covered her mouth to stifle a laugh.

"I'm sorry," vaguely he heard Mary say. She tried wiping his shirt with her bare hands. He brushed her aside. "Get away from me. You ...!" He hurried to the bathroom.

Urbo and Manwo were now roaring, holding their sides. "It's me, Urbo!" Harry heard the bathroom door open and close. "Are you okay?"

"Stay away from me," sneered Harry. "No! I'm not!" He bent his head under the faucet and washed his mouth out.

"It was an accident." Urbo had a hard time keeping a straight face. "Mary wouldn't do a thing like that on purpose." He couldn't hold out any longer, thinking about the expression on Harry's face when Mary had puked on him.

"Why me?" Harry pounded his fist down on the sink.

"No big deal," replied Urbo. "She didn't do it on purpose. She's real scared that you won't forgive her."

"I bet," replied Harry, more embarrassed than angry.

"It was an accident, and she's sorry, Harry. What more can I say to convince you? Nobody could plan anything as rotten as that!"

Harry pulled off his shirt and wiped himself clean. "Just leave me alone," he pouted. "If you want to help, just leave me be."

"Here, I brought you a clean shirt." Urbo held it out. "Take it, Harry; don't be a spoil sport. You'll ruin the day for everyone."

"You expect me to go out there and pretend that nothing happened?"

"You don't have to pretend anything. You have to get it through that thick skull of yours that it was an accident and accidents happen. Right?"

"Maybe."

"Mary likes you a whole lot. And you have to admit that everything was going good for you until she got sick. You were almost in her pants."

"Hmm..."

"Whatta say?" He saw Harry wavering. "Come on."

"I don't know."

"You were almost in her pants? Weren't you?"

"Yeh."

"Then she must like you a whole lot. Right?"

"Yeh."

"Then you'll go out and forgive her?" Urbo didn't give Harry time to think. He took him by the arm and led him back into the living room.

"O Harry," exclaimed Mary as soon as she saw him. "I'm sorry! Seems that I'm always hurting you somehow. Forgive me?"

Harry hesitated for effect. "Yeh…" He suddenly replied. "I guess so."

"Oh Harry," Mary rushed into his arms. "You're the nicest, kindest, most gentle man I have ever known." She stroked his ego.

"Hey, you two," Manwo interrupted. "I hate to break you two up, but if we plan to be on time, we better get moving. It's getting late."

"Let's go!" Mary slid her arm through Harry's and followed after Manwo and Urbo.

— CHAPTER SEVEN —

By nine o'clock in the morning on any weekday, the streets of New York are bumper to bumper with traffic. It's madness!

Harry inhaled deeply. His nose twitched.

"Something the matter?" Mary asked, sitting next to him in the back seat of Urbo's Volkswagen.

"Nothing the matter," he replied. "Ever since I was a little kid, I've liked the smell of bus fumes."

"Oh...?" What was Mary to say to that? She shifted restlessly.

"Me, too," Manwo turned round in the front seat. "You ever sniffed any glue?"

"No..."

"If you get off on exhaust fumes, you'll love the high you get from sniffing glue."

"You two live together?" asked Harry out of the blue.

"Yes," replied Manwo. "We've been partners for a world's record for both of us. Almost a year. How about you? Where you living?"

"I'm staying with my parents, he replied, "until I can find a place of my own."

"Won't your folks be uptight that you didn't come home last night?" Manwo asked.

"They won't do anything crazy like calling the police to find you?" Urbo asked with a trace of nervousness in his voice.

"Na..." Harry waved his hand. "You see, I come from a big family. I got me ten brothers and sisters. My folks have plenty to worry about. They're used to me by now. I've been an independent person all my life. When you come from a big family like I do, you learn soon enough to take care of yourself. You know, when I was only sixteen years old, between my junior and senior year in high school, my dad thought it was time for me to see what a slice of life on my own was all about. School had recessed for the summer, and father drove me out to the interstate and gave me a hundred dollars. He patted me on the back and said that he would see me in the fall before school opened."

"He did?" Manwo leaned further into the back seat. "What did you do next?"

"I hitched my way cross-country to California. I pitched hay for meals and picked cucumbers for a dollar a day. In San Francisco, I got me this job on the wharves, but that didn't last too long. Two of the biggest guys you ever seen took their miseries out on me. A prime example of being at the right place at the wrong time. They laid me up in the hospital with broken ribs for over a week. When I was discharged, I decided the better part of valor was not to go back."

Urbo laughed. "Now that was smart of you, I like a man who's smart enough not to make the same mistake twice. Brains," he poked his head. "Is what separates man from the rest of the animals."

"What did you do after you got out of the hospital?" Mary was impressed by Harry's story.

"I washed dishes, swept floors, cleaned out toilets, anything to stay alive."

"You're a survivor," Urbo smiled at him through the rearview mirror. "I like you. And I wouldn't say that if I didn't mean it. Ask Manwo."

"That's the truth," she replied.

"It must be wonderful to come from a large, loving family," said Mary, melancholy.

"My parents," said Mary. "I never knew my mother. She ran off with some trombone player soon after she gave birth to me. So says my father, anyways."

"You get to see your father often?" asked Harry.

"No more," she replied. "Dad came home one day early from work and caught me in bed with another woman. He freaked out and threw me out of the house. Said I was like my mother!"

"What?"

"You're surprised to hear that I swing both ways?"

"Me! No! No!" Harry tried appearing suave. "I know lots of girls who are AC/DC."

Urbo laughed. "We should get your father and my mother together. Now me, I've been to so many weddings where my mother was the bride; it's coming out of my ears."

"Know what you mean," said Manwo, rubbing Urbo's neck. "I'm never going to get married."

"Me either," agreed Urbo.

"Well... I'd kinda like to myself," sweetly said Mary. "Get married, have a big family like Harry. I think that's real swell."

"Oh, you silly kitten," Manwo teased. "You know very well that no one man or woman could satisfy you."

"Stop that!" Mary snapped. "Don't say that!"

"Why not?" Manwo stroked her arm. "It's the truth, isn't it?"

"Stop your gaming, you two," yelled Urbo. "Don't we have enough to worry about, without you two at each other's throats?"

"Don't be upset." Manwo saw Harry twitching uneasily. "Me and Mary are like sisters. And like brothers, we're always at each other. Neither of us means anything."

Around and around the same block drove Urbo. "At this rate, we ain't going to find a parking space till the sun goes down over the Federal Building."

"Every day a new sun is born," said Harry from out of nowhere.

"What...?"

"I mean, every day a new sun is born. At night, it glows and breaks up into little pieces, floating away on their own to make the stars we see on a rare night here in New York."

"You're crazier than shit," laughed Urbo.

"I am not," flamed Harry through slitted eyes. "I'm as sane as any of you."

"You're a romantic," replied Urbo. "And anyone who's a romantic these days has to be nuts."

"You can't fool me," Mary snuggled closer. "I'm surprised at you, after all you have done and experienced in life. I would have never guessed it of you."

Urbo, irritated by the traffic, yelled, "Hold on!" He pressed down on the accelerator. "I'm sick of this messing around," he mumbled. "Out of my way, Urbo's coming through!"

"I hope the pigs do something stupid," Manwo reached between her legs and came up with a World War Two helmet. "Let 'em try! Just let 'em, I'm ready." She popped it on.

"Put that down!" yelled Urbo. "You crazy too? You want to get us all busted?" He saw an opening and pressed between a bus and a truck into a parking space.

"I thought you guys said there wasn't going to be any trouble?" Harry leaned backwards, cracking his knuckles.

"We did," replied Urbo, turning off the engine. "There won't be any unless the pigs start it first. But we do have the right and the obligation to ourselves to be ready to defend ourselves in case. We do have that right, don't we, Harry?"

"I guess so, but I don't think..."

"You think too much! That's your problem," said Manwo. "Let's get going, or we'll miss all the action."

"Don't forget the stuff. And remember," Urbo wagged a finger at Manwo, "that we don't want to be drawing attention to ourselves. Let the others get the publicity. We got a job to do."

"Point that finger at somebody else," Manwo pushed it aside.

"Who in the hell do you think you are? Who planned this job, anyways?"

Angrily, she opened the door and jumped out.

Mary hurried after, running to catch up.

"Say, Urbo," Harry stumbled out of the car. "What's Manwo have in that bag?"

"A surprise," he grinned. "Hey, listen!" He cupped his ear. "Can you hear? 'Down with the President! Save the environment! No more strip mining! Stop the killing of the whales! Down with the Jewish capitalist!'"

Urbo and Harry ran to catch up with the ladies.

"Look," Manwo pointed. "There must be a thousand people in front of the Federal Building."

"Yes...!"

"I told you guys there would be a big turnout. It looks like the others are riling the crowd up good."

"That's what we need!"

Harry was feeling uncomfortable about the way his new friends were acting. He didn't feel so good. What was the problem? What were they protesting? He didn't know; he didn't care. It had nothing to do with him.

"Hey you guys!" Nervous perspiration dripped in a circle under Harry's armpits. "You think we should go over there? It looks to me like some of your friends are going to cause trouble."

Urbo laid a heavy hand on Harry's shoulder. He squeezed. "We haven't the time to explain everything to you now, old buddy!" He glared.

"You have to make a choice. Either you're with the people or you're against us. There isn't any middle ground in this war!"

"Of course he's with us!" Mary stepped to Harry's defense. "Let's go." She pulled him away from Urbo.

"What does Manwo have in that bag?" he asked again.

"It's a surprise, like Urbo said. It's nothing!"

"Nothing! Nothing! Then why is everyone afraid to tell me?"

"I give you my word that nothing but good will come out of it. You trust me?"

"Yes, I trust you. I...I...just don't want to get into any more trouble. Been in enough lately. Don't know if I could take any more."

"Harry, I swear to you on a stack of Bibles," she crossed her heart, "that if there's any trouble, we won't be the ones who start it. Harry? You hear me?"

"Yes, I hear you. You said that there won't be any trouble." He thought sullenly to himself, 'I don't want to lose her.'

"I'm with you," he replied not too happily. "All the way."

Skippy do da, skippy day, young lovers strolling on a summer's day. Out to make the world a better place to live in.

***

Out in front of the Federal Building stood the demonstrators nose to nose with the police—dressed in full battle gear, nightsticks at the ready, standing motionless, taking the taunting of the demonstrators without flinching. From out of the crowd, a rock came flying, hitting a police officer smack in the head. Down he went, grabbing hold of his head, blood already seeping through his fingers. The officer next to him acted by reflex. He swung his club at the first person he set eyes on. The crowd became furious. Another rock came hurling at the police, then another and another. The police charged. The demonstrators fought back. A riot broke out. A shot went off. A split second of quiet laid over both the police and the demonstrators.

Breaking out of their trance first, the crowd broke and ran. The police were at their heels, striking anyone who wasn't wearing a uniform. Dozens were wounded, laying bleeding on the pavement.

"Okay, let's get going." Urbo ordered the others to follow him. He led them down an alley in the opposite direction, away from the scene of the riot.

"Hey!" protested Harry, stopping suddenly in his tracks. "I thought you said there wasn't going to be any trouble? You promised!" trembling, he gaped at Mary.

"Shut your mouth," snapped Manwo. "Now's not the time to be arguing. You want to get us all busted?" She nervously glanced around.

Harry allowed Mary to lead him off down the alley. Urbo led, coming to a halt back on the busy street. "Walk naturally," he said out of the side of his mouth.

Harry felt the tension running between them. He couldn't take his eyes off the little brown bag Manwo carried. The street was crowded with people heading in every direction. To the stranger, it would have looked like there weren't any rules for the traffic of pedestrians and cars. For some ten minutes, they walked quite quickly, fitting into the picture with no problems. Then Urbo stopped and took the bag away from Manwo. He opened the zipper and fooled around inside for a few seconds. "There, it's all set," he handed the bag back. "Good luck! You know what to do."

Manwo slipped off her trench coat, and to Harry's surprise, she was wearing a dress underneath. She smiled. "Now or never!" She took a deep breath.

"Wish me luck." She handed her coat to Mary and slowly walked across the street. She disappeared into the Bank of America.

"What's she up to now?" worriedly said Harry. "What we stopping here for? I thought we were trying to escape from the police."

"She's stashing the bag in a safety deposit box we rented earlier in case of an emergency," replied Urbo. "For safekeeping till it's safe to come back and get it."

"Hmm...?"

"Where is she?" Urbo tapped his foot impatiently, constantly looking back over his shoulder.

"Don't want to get stopped by the cops and have anything

on us that we could get busted on. Don't get me wrong. I don't expect…"

"Hold it," exclaimed Mary. "There she is now."

"Easy, everybody!" Urbo ordered them to nonchalantly move down the street. Manwo angled across the street to cut them off. "Smooth," she said, her eyes glazed with excitement. "Let's get the hell out of here!"

"We have three minutes," said Urbo, already moving off.

"Wait a minute," Harry stamped his foot. "Wait one damn minute!"

"You wait a minute," hissed Manwo. "That bank's set to blow in less than three minutes. I don't know what you're going to do, but I'm getting the hell out of here." She ran after Urbo.

"Mary?" he pleaded. "You said…?"

"I'm sorry, Harry. It was for the people." She said nothing more and fled after the others.

"Mary!… Mary!…" yelled Harry. "Mary…! Mary…! No…!" he screamed, muffled by the explosion. It rippled down the street, shattering department store windows for five blocks around. Police sirens ringing, traffic snarled by one driver running into another, injured bystanders cut by flying glass— one little girl laid in the middle of the sidewalk in a pool of blood.

Torn between staying where he was and fleeing for his good-for-nothing life, he fled. He raced round the corner running as fast as he could, running on impulse engines till he thought he was safe. Off in the distance, he could still hear the sirens wailing. He wondered how the little girl was doing and prayed that she wasn't too seriously injured. From the direction he came from, he saw smoke rising over the tops of skyscrapers. He worried about starting a fire that would burn the city down. He hated New York but didn't want to hurt anyone. He worried again about the pretty little pretty girl and convinced himself that she was dead. It was his fault. He was a murderer.

"Oh my God!" he anguished. "Dozens of people must

have been killed in the bank. All those poor innocents, their families, and friends!" He frantically tried to think about what he was to do next.

He couldn't go home. That was the first place the police would search for him. And for certain he wasn't going to go back to Mary's apartment. He felt bitter towards her and scared of the others. He had no one to turn to, no friends or acquaintances. He searched through his pockets. His pants were soaked through with perspiration. He pulled out a handful of crumpled bills. He counted, "Ten, fifteen, sixteen dollars and change. Not much," he shrugged. "But it's going to have to do."

He stepped to the curb and waved a cab down. "Where to?"

"Grand Central Station," he replied, jittery. "And hurry if you please. I'm already late for my train."

"You hear about the trouble downtown?" The cabbie made idle conversation.

"What trouble?" Harry played it cool.

"There was a riot in front of the Federal Building. I heard from one of my passengers that a couple of demonstrators were shot by the police."

"No kidding?" Nervously, Harry looked out the window.

"Yes, and a few blocks away, some nuts blew up the Bank of America. Can you believe that? I hope they catch the bastards. Better dead, I say, than alive!"

Harry shifted uneasily. His wet pants were riding up his legs, sticking, itching his ass.

"I heard over the radio," the driver, Harry, could see, was clearly enraged, "that a dozen people were seriously injured and taken to the hospital. Some of them in critical condition. The bastards! I'd sure like to get my hands on whoever's responsible."

Harry's knees knocked. "Oh…Oh…" pounded his heart.

"I'd blow their heads off, yeah! That's what I'd do with them radicals. I'd cut 'em up in little pieces. I'd do it very slowly."

Harry rubbed his throat, wishing he'd hurry.

"Probably, I'd bet," the cabbie drove forward, daring anyone but a truck to get in his way. "It was those damn militant Jews!" He pulled up in front of the train station.

"Here we are. That will be four bucks."

Harry saw the cab driver push the meter ahead an extra fifty cents, but he didn't want to cause any trouble for himself. "Here." He handed him what he had asked.

"Thanks!" On top, he gave him another dollar tip.

Inside the station, he headed straight to get his ticket. "When's the next train leaving?" he asked the clerk.

"Depends on where you want to go," he replied.

"Anywhere," replied Harry, sweating heavily. "Just so it's the next one out, I don't care."

"The next train due to depart is bound for the Jersey Shore. That okay?"

"That will do nicely."

"One way or round trip?"

"One way."

"That will be nine dollars and thirty-three cents."

On the way through the station, he stopped and bought a few candy bars to take on the train. He was so conscious of appearing normal that he fumbled and dropped and miscounted his money till everyone around was laughing at him. He hurried away without waiting for his change. Once on board, he found a seat in the rear where he could keep an eye on the comings and goings of the other passengers. To his relief, the train started moving on time. "Thank God!" He mumbled under his breath. "First piece of good luck I've had all day."

"Pardon me!"

How long could a good thing last? Harry stared up at an impeccably groomed gentleman dressed in a grey pinstriped suit. His hair was perfect. His shirt showed at his coat sleeve, just right. His shoes were brown Florsheim's. The knot in his tie was large and tight.

"Pardon me," the stranger smiled. "Is this seat taken?"

Harry scratched his forehead, looking through his fingers down the aisle. 'Why this seat?' he thought suspiciously. The carriage was practically empty.

"No," he replied, standing up and letting the man slide by to his seat.

"Hi," said the stranger as he sat down.

"Hi," Harry tried to sound unfriendly, forcing himself to look away.

"You going down to the Shore on vacation?"

"You could say that."

"Me too. My daughter and a few friends rented a house for the summer in Deal, New Jersey. They've invited me down for a few days of rest and relaxation."

"Hmm..." rudely Harry mumbled. "That's nice." Paranoia invaded him being himself.

"My name's Hamish Zahari. What's yours?"

Harry wanted to crush his mouth into pieces and scream for him to stop questioning him. But instead, he was frightened that the man would get suspicious if he hesitated any longer. He blurted, "Harry!" His voice cracked.

"Well, Harry, glad to make your acquaintance." He saw Harry pale as a ghost. "You feeling okay?"

"Fine, I'm feeling fine. A little uptight, maybe. Just finished my exams and haven't slept for a few days. That's all."

Harry felt sick, alright. His stomach churned juices, his mouth tasted of sour milk, he felt hot all over, and when he closed his eyes hoping that maybe the stranger would be quiet if he saw him resting, his head started spinning. Harry's feeling tumbled, humming high on fear, his senses overcooking. Everywhere he looked, he saw a threat. His underwear sticking between the cracks of his cheeks, he squirmed in his seat.

"You sure you're feeling okay?" concerned, Hamish

asked once again.

"Sure," he replied. "Hey? What's the train slowing down for? I thought they said this was an express?" His imagination broke loose.

He thought that the train was stopping so the police could come on board and arrest him.

"It is," replied Hamish. "We're down at the Shore. From here on in, we stop at every little resort."

"Down at the Shore? Already?" He couldn't believe it. He was scared. "Now what am I going to do?"

"Where you getting off at?"

"Oh, I don't know. I'm bumming around for the time being, I guess."

"In my time," replied Hamish, "I did a whole lot of traveling myself. Some people call that idleness. I say for some people, it's absolutely necessary to be free to come and go, be, and happen as you please for a while. Get your head together, as you people would say." He chuckled over himself, enjoying showing others he knew where it was at.

"I guess so." Harry really didn't want to talk to him anymore. He decided he would chance it and get off at the next stop.

"Listen," said Hamish, bound and determined to rescue Harry whether he wanted to be rescued or not. "Maybe it's none of my business. I know that we've only known each other a short time. But honestly, you don't look so good to me."

'Oh, shut up,' Harry screamed to himself. 'Shut your big trap! Please!'

"My stop is next." Hamish didn't or wouldn't take any of his cues. "I was thinking, considering you don't haven't any destination in mind, would you consider coming along to my daughter's place with me? I'm sure you'll be welcomed. You can get some rest and a good meal down, and whenever you're feeling up to it again, you can go on your way."

"Oh..." Harry was taken back, suspicious still of the

stranger's motives. "Oh… I don't know if I should."

"Why not? What's stopping you? You said that you don't haven't any other plans." He persisted. "Have you?"

"No…"

"You need the rest, and I guarantee you a fantastic meal."

'What's with this guy?' Harry thought about the others he had trusted and where that had led him. "Why are you going to all this bother over me?"

"I gathered you are Jewish," replied Hamish, matter-of-factly. "You are? Aren't you?"

"Yes! So what?"

"So, a lot of things to me. I'm the representative for Hebrew University in the United States. It's part of my job to be interested in every Jewish man or woman. Obviously, you are Jewish if I know," proudly added Hamish. "I'm famous among my friends and acquaintances for being able to spot a Jew out of a crowd. Hardly ever wrong."

"That's some trick." For Harry, it had been some time since he had last admitted to anyone that he was Jewish. He felt cold guilt in his chest, facing this man who was so obviously proud of his heritage.

"Well, how about it?" Hamish wouldn't let go.

"How about what?" Harry played coy.

"Stopping over at my daughter's house till you're feeling up to yourself?" Hamish felt that patience was a virtue he sometimes stretched thin. "Think it over, Harry. We have a few minutes before my stop comes up."

Gathering together bits and pieces of clues, Hamish surmised that Harry was in some kind of trouble. Added to that, why was he so reluctant to admit he was a Jew? Not so unusual. He was afraid among his American brethren. He reaffirmed his resolve to help Harry if allowed. The conductor came into the car. "Deal, Deal, New Jersey! Next stop!" He announced in a baritone voice, walking rapidly between the rows of seats.

"That's me, said Hamish. "Excuse me." He slid by. "Have

you made your mind up yet?"

"Hmm...?" Harry would have felt better about going along if only he knew the real reasons why Hamish was being so kind. He was thankful that Hamish had tried. 'If it wasn't for bad luck,' Harry's guts kicked the walls of his stomach, 'I wouldn't have any luck at all!'

"I'd better not!" He watched Hamish slip on his coat. "I don't think I'd better," he said. "I kinda want to travel alone for a while. Pull it together, you know."

Screeching its brakes, the train slid to a stop, reminding Harry of his Aunt Gracie's voice. Hamish glanced out the window. "Hey!" He exclaimed, "There's my daughter." He waved, "Deborah!"

He hesitated before leaving. "You sure?" He figured he'd give Harry one last chance to change his mind.

"I'm sorry, but I don't think I ought to."

"Sure?"

"Ye..."

"Have it your own way," replied Hamish, not hiding his disappointment. "It's been nice passing the time with you." He shook Harry's hand. "I sure wish you'd change your mind."

"No, but thanks anyways."

Harry watched Hamish get off the train. 'Maybe I should've.' He wavered.

***

The train made a great deal of noise pulling away from the depot. Hamish was greeted enthusiastically by his daughter. She threw her arms around him. He lifted her off the ground and swung her around.

He let her down, and as soon as her feet were on the ground, Hamish turned serious. "Are the others here yet?"

"They're here," she replied. "Is everything all right?" As close as she was to her father, she picked up right away that something was amiss.

69

"We have problems," he replied. "That's our lot. But truthfully, yes. I met this fellow on the train. He upset me." He took her arm. "I'll tell you about him on the way home."

"Trouble?"

"No trouble," he replied, glancing over his shoulder. "Hold on!" Hamish stopped suddenly surprised. "You see that man standing over there?"

"Yes," Deborah replied, picking her heart up from the pit of her stomach.

"That's the guy I was talking about... Wait here for a second. I'll see what he wants."

Walking with a smile, waving his hand. "Harry," he hollered across the tracks. "You've changed your mind?"

"If your offer is still open?" he hollered back. "I'm not feeling very well."

"Sure! Terrific! I don't mean that I'm happy you're sick. Oh, never mind!"

Hamish stopped in the middle of the tracks and waited for Harry to meet him halfway.

"You sure it's okay?" Harry stumbled.

Grabbing hold of him before he fell over. "Sure," he steadied Harry. "Sure, I'm sure. Let's go; I'll introduce you to my daughter."

Contrasting with Harry frowning, Hamish was grinning from ear to ear. "Deborah, I would like you to meet a friend of mine. He'll be staying with us for a few days if it's okay with you?"

"That will be fine." She didn't know what else to say under the circumstances.

"Harry, I want you to say hello to the delight of my life. My daughter, Deborah. She's as brilliant as she is beautiful."

"Oh, father," replied Deborah, pretending embarrassment. "It's nice to meet you, Harry," she said nicely. "Any friend of father's is naturally a friend of mine. Have you have any luggage?"

"No…" He replied uneasily. "I travel light."

"Harry's not feeling too well," said Hamish. "He has the flu or something. I think the best thing for him is a warm, comfortable bed."

"We have that," she replied. "Right this way. I parked the car a couple of blocks from here." She thought to herself, leading them out of the depot, that the others weren't going to like her father bringing a stranger into the house.

— CHAPTER EIGHT —

Sitting between father and daughter squeezed Harry. He was feeling uneasy about going into a stranger's home, wishing he had stayed on the train, going his own way. But to where? That was the problem and the reason he was going along.

"Any news from home?" Deborah drove carefully with both hands on the steering wheel.

"A lot," replied Hamish. "All the same old crap! The government's uneasy about the assassination attempts on American Jews! Israel's the only nation I know where everyone thinks they're the prime minister. There are millions of people in Israel, more coming every day. And each and every one of us has a different point of view. We have so many different viewpoints going about that we're always sticking each other up the old arse. You ever hear of a crazy old coot called Yeshaayia Gurevich?"

"Sure," Deborah replied. "He's another one of those fanatics running around claiming the Messiah is coming. The end-of-the-world crap! So? Nobody ever pays any of them any attention."

"Some do," replied Hamish. "It seems that quite a few people are paying attention to this Gurevich. Some fanatic Rabbi named Tzadikovich and his congregation have organized demonstrations, riling up some of the right-wing religious elements in the country. Big trouble, I tell you, is brewing. I feel it in these bones of mine. The pot is boiling, and if the Arabs and the Communists don't drive us into an early grave, like rats with no place to go, we're about to blow. It's madness."

***

Standing on a corner outside the Me'ah She'arim Quarter, searching every passing face for Har Megiddo, Yeshaayia Gurevich had plenty of guilt piled high on his shoulders. In his own eyes, he was a failure. He saw himself as others viewed him: ridiculous, dangerous. He had failed the Lord, failed himself, and failed all his loved ones. He thought of himself as a prideful man and because of this, the Messiah refused to show his face to him.

No matter how badly he felt, how terribly the day had gone, or how hungry, bone-aching, and heart-sobbing he felt, a smile digs in and radiates from his face.

He had left the desert for Jerusalem many hours before the sun showed its glory. Now it was long past its bedtime. He was about to call it a day and head back to the desert when, off in the distance, he heard loud shouting coming his way. He waited; curiosity held him fast.

Trembling from the night's chill, he sneezed. He did not bother to wipe his nose. His attention was taken by a conversation going on behind him.

"Here comes that maniac Tzadikovich and his crazier-than-a-loon followers."

"What in the heck are they protesting now? That our country's armed forces are working on the Sabbath?"

"Who knows?" replied the other angrily. "To tell you the truth, I'm getting pretty sick of the whole bunch of them. The government should lock 'em up. I heard from a friend who has a friend whose wife is a dispatcher at police headquarters that the Neturei Karta's are giving aid and comfort to the Arab terrorists."

"I wouldn't doubt that for a second. Anyways, who the hell is this Har Megiddo that the old Rabbi keeps jabbering about? What the devil has he done?"

"Oh, it's not Megiddo the Rabbi's after. He says that this Megiddo doesn't exist! What the Rabbi wants is for the authorities to lock up some other fanatic named Gurevich who preaches that Har Megiddo is the Messiah."

Yeshaayia hid his face in the crook of his arm, sure that if someone saw him smiling, they would know who he was.

"That again! Don't we have enough trouble in Israel? More tumult than we can barely handle, and these people are demonstrating, wasting their time and effort on a Messiah that we've been waiting for three thousand years. Bah! Humbug! The whole lot of them are fools!"

"I say we should throw the whole lot of them in a dungeon, throw away the key, and good riddance!"

"And if the government won't take stronger measures, I say that doesn't leave the rest of us much choice. We should take matters into our own hands!"

"I agree!"

Yeshaayia breathed deeply, held it, trying to shrink himself. He started to move away before he was recognized in the middle of the street, standing on the white line, his legs rubbery, turning a deaf ear to the commands coming from his head to move.

Down the street came Rabbi Tzadikovich, coming down the line directly at Yeshaayia, leading a small but vocal and rowdy mob, blocking traffic for blocks behind. Yeshaayia told himself to run, but he couldn't lift a foot. Closer and closer they came. Hiding his face under his arm, crouched low, horns blasting, drivers threatening the marchers, small Arab boys throwing sticks and stones, and their parents' yelling obscenities. Walking shoulder to shoulder with the Rabbi on the one side was Mordecai, and on the other, Yeshaayia's daughter Rachel. She carried a megaphone in her hand and was now pressing it to her lips.

"I am the daughter of the false prophet Yeshaayia Gurevich. I bear witness to my father's desecration of the Lord's Teachings. I bear witness to his use of the Lord's name in vain for the Devil's own evil purposes. I bear witness to his collaboration with the enemies of our people!"

"No...!" pained poor Yeshaayia. "No..." He tried yelling to Rachel that it wasn't true, but nothing more than a groan came out in the place of his protest.

Magor, who followed behind the Rabbi and in front of the other elders, saw Yeshaayia first and hollered. "There, Rabbi! There he is! The Devil's advocate here on earth,

74

Yeshaayia Gurevich!"

"There he is!" another Guardian screamed. "Over there, that's him! I knew him in the old days!"

Yeshaayia, stunned stone-still except for his knees knocking together, with great effort stretched his hands towards his daughter.

Stunned as much as he was, barely audibly Rachel gasped, "Father…!" Her heart pumping, her body trembling, she hesitatingly stepped forward a few steps.

"Father…? Is that really you...?" She knew it was but couldn't believe that this man with the ugly open sores was him. "God!"

The followers of the Rabbi waited for some signal from their leader, whispering and pointing at Yeshaayia. Rabbi Tzadikovich reached out and grabbed Rachel before she could go any further.

"Mordecai," he scowled. "Take your wife home. Now!" He hollered because Mordecai had not moved fast enough to suit him.

"Noo..." Rachel tried breaking the Rabbi's hold. "Father!" she screamed, "What have they, we, you done to yourself?"

"Rachel!" Tzadikovich shook her. "Rachel!" he hollered. "Rachel!" He slapped her across the face. "You've done your duty! Be sure God will reward you. Now go home!"

Her head snapped, her ears rang, her cheek turned a bluish black, and her senses scattered in no sensible direction.

"Go home," Rabbi Tzadikovich yelled and tossed her into Mordecai's arms. "I hold you responsible," he pointed a finger at him, "that your wife goes straight home and stays there till I can find the time to pay you a visit."

Mordecai cowered under the Rabbi's barrage. He gathered his sobbing, hysterical, wisp of a wife in his arms and walked her slowly through the demonstrators. The Rabbi watched them disappear, then he turned his attention back to the hated Yeshaayia.

"Now I have you in the limelight, you worm, you pig!" The Rabbi's mind spat mud.

"The right hand of the devil!" he screamed, overwrought. "See how he shakes. He is cursed by God for selling his soul to the Zionists." His fat face turned beet red. "Look, he smiles at us. He mocks us Guardians. Remember this dog. Burn his face in your minds. Remember, if ever you should think about straying from the path of righteousness, this," he pointed at Yeshaayia, "is your fate!"

"Down with the blasphemer! Down with the accursed one!" Magor picked up the chant started by the Cantor, immediately joined by the rest of the Guardians. They stamped their feet, shouting at the top of their lungs.

They surrounded Yeshaayia on all sides. He prayed to shrink into nothing. He fell to his knees. They taunted, threatened, spat, and picked and pulled at his already tattered clothes. Their faces were distorted into terrible, ugly clown faces. Smeared lipstick on their lips, powder blotted, rouge smudged, eyebrows thick and sticky, terrible rage pulling their skin taut.

"It's the police," one of the Guardians hollered a warning. "Run for it!" This caused the others to panic.

Mager ran to the Rabbi's side and urged him to leave. "Hurry!" But the Rabbi paid him no mind, not being able to tear his eyes off Yeshaayia. As the police chased after the demonstrators, they knocked Yeshaayia over on his face and ran up and down his back. What took so long to build up was over in a matter of minutes. The police arrested as many demonstrators as they could catch. Through pained eyes, Yeshaayia saw the police taking the Rabbi away. He did not resist. He went along without a fuss, his cold eyes peering over his shoulder at Yeshaayia, who held his stare for as long as he could. Beaten, he lowered his eyes.

Rabbi Tzadikovich laughed harshly, cruelly, flipped his head in disdain of Yeshaayia, and disappeared into a waiting police van. Yeshaayia pulled himself up to a sitting position. There were still bystanders muddling around. No one noticed the old man sitting in the middle of the street. No one offered to help him up. Cars roared by on either side as if he were part and parcel of the road. He pulled himself up on his feet. Horns blasting. People are leaning out of their car windows, yelling for him to get out of the street. After a few near misses, he wobbled over to the sidewalk and leaned on a lamp post. He was still smiling.

***

Rabbi Tzadikovich was taken to police headquarters and charged with disorderly conduct and inciting a riot.

"Well, at least that dog Yeshaayia is out in the open again." He pondered this evening's events in retrospect. 'Surprised me that we drove him out so soon. Could have handled the situation better if I was ready, but all things considered, winging it, all went fair to middlin'... "Except"— he' had an afterthought. 'I should have listened to Magor and left before I was arrested. 'That was stupid!'

The Rabbi pondered and pondered, searched his head for how he could turn being jailed from a defeat into his advantage. He scratched his head, the dandruff falling on his black coat. He was getting nowhere except rubbing the skin off the back of his neck when he heard his cell door open and the jailer bringing him his supper.

"Is this kosher?" he asked in a gruff, unfriendly voice.

"Of course it is, Rabbi," replied the jailer. "What kind of place do you think we run here?"

"I don't believe you," retorted the Rabbi. "Take this food out of here," he ordered.

As the door clanged shut, leaving him alone, he had an idea.

***

In the morning newspapers, it hit the public that all the demonstrators arrested the previous night had been set free on bond—all except one. Their leader, Rabbi Tzadikovich, who had refused food or water, had said he would fast in jail till the authorities arrested Yeshaayia Gurevich for his crimes.

Rabbi Tzadikovich claimed that Gurevich was responsible for the many terrorist murders that had taken place in Israel. He alleged that Gurevich, under the false cover of the Zionist cause, was using the name Har Megiddo as a front to hide his crimes against the Jewish people. "Zionist and Nazi!" he called him. The Rabbi said that he was adamant that he would neither take food nor drink till the authorities met his demands.

When asked if he meant his threat to death, he replied that whether he lived or died made little difference. What was important was that the Jewish people should see the false prophet for what he was—the greatest menace to our very survival we had ever had. Greater than Hitler! Greater than all the Hitlers we had ever had to contend with in our long, arduous history. He called on all good Jews from all over the world. He asked for the help of all peoples, non-Jews and Jews alike, to tear down the flag of Israel and keep the heritage of the chosen people safe till the Lord should see fit to send his spirit to gather the people under David's banner.

A spokesman for the government replied to the statements of the Rabbi by saying the government had no reason to arrest Yeshaayia Gurevich. "Until he breaks the law, he will be treated with the rights and privileges justly due him under the laws of the state."

The spokesman added that he saw the actions of the Rabbi as being divisive. He called for the Rabbi to break his fast immediately. He announced that the government would have no further comments on the 'incident,' as he called it. The Rabbi stuck by his fast, now going into its second day. Thereafter, each day, the newspapers, radio, and television counted the days of the fast for the public. "Give the fat to the poor," one commentator sickly joked. The Rabbi, Yeshaayia, and Har Megiddo became household names in Israel. Little by little, the news of the three and their struggle leaked out and filtered round the world. As of this time, the world had little reason to pay much attention.

— CHAPTER NINE —

"Poor Harry isn't at all well, father. He's running a slight fever; his teeth are chattering, so he's cut his poor lips to pieces. The things I've done—the pills, cold towels on his forehead, mentholatum rub on his chest and back. Covered him with blankets, hoping he'll sweat the cold out of himself during the night."

Famished, the seagulls were uttering their guttural cries, swooping down on the garbage left on the beaches by the sun worshippers.

"You've done as much as humanly possible," replied Hamish. If he isn't feeling better by morning, you can take him back to the city to see a doctor."

"That's fine, but what I don't understand is why you brought a stranger into the house at a time like this? Haven't we enough tsuris on our hands?"

"He's a Jew," replied Hamish, thinking that that said it all. "I'd appreciate it very much if you and the others would try and be nice to him."

"I've tried, and I'm sure that Ashel and Al will too. But you still haven't answered my question fully."

"I thought I had."

"He's a Jew and lost his way, and you've appointed yourself to guide him home to the Holy Land. Is that what you're telling me?"

"Something like that," he replied. "I have this feeling about him. He's most secretive about something."

"I know, I know. You don't have to tell me; he's a touchy devil. I asked him what his last name was, and he bit my head off."

"Have a little patience. Israel needs all the men and women she can lay her hands on."

"No denying that. Okay, I could never say no to you. I

promise I'll do my best to be nice, but he doesn't make it easy."

"Do your best. I or no one else can ask any more."

"That reminds me," said Deborah. "Ashel and Al were anxious to see you. Have you seen them yet?"

"I saw them for a few minutes after I arrived."

"And...?"

"As always, as I said in the car, there's always trouble for Jews. I think it ironic that the Jews stepped out of the Holocaust right into the eye of a storm."

"Yes... And...?"

"Intelligence has confirmed what we've known for a long time. That the Arabs have trained and financed foreigners to come to the United States and assassinate some of the most influential Jews in America."

"Do we know who's on their list?"

"Lists, you mean, and to answer your question - we can make an educated guess."

"Do the Americans know?"

"They have been informed, but they're not taking it too seriously."

"They're getting smug with their power," replied Deborah. "And us? We're taking it seriously, aren't we?"

"We're taking it very seriously. That's why I'm here in the States. I've been sent with orders to do what's necessary to foil it, if possible—to protect our people at all costs."

"Figures."

"What figures?" Hamish yawned. He hadn't slept a wink in almost a week.

"That the Americans sit on their backsides while Jews are threatened and murdered."

"Why so harsh? The American people have been kind and generous to us."

"Don't be so harsh? Unbelievable!" she retorted. "I just don't understand your attitude. The President is an outright anti-

Semite. He barely hid his true feelings during the election campaign. It has become socially and politically popular now for the liberals to support the Arabs, no matter what the rights or wrongs of a situation may be."

"You're being unreasonable."

"I am! How can you say that? Why can't you admit to the simple truth? The United States is selling us out for the black gold the Arabs have under their deserts."

"I admit to nothing I can't agree with," sighed Hamish. "I say the Americans are in a funny position. They're our only friends in the world, and God knows what will become of us if they pull their support away. No... What we must do is work harder to strengthen our bonds of friendship with the American government—but, more importantly, with the American people. And if we allow their sentiments to change, that is our fault."

"I love you very much." Deborah saw how tired her father was. "Even though I don't always agree with you," she laughed.

"I don't know what I would have done without you," he replied. "When you laugh, you remind me so much of your dear departed mother."

"What would I have done without you?" She stroked her father's temple. "You look beat, Dad." She said "Dad" when she felt most tender towards him.

"I am," he yawned again. "I was hoping to catch a few winks before I met with the brothers."

"Stretch out. Up with your legs." She massaged his calves. "I'll wake you in plenty of time."

Hamish fell asleep. In a few minutes, he was snoring away.

***

Harry woke in the morning stuck to the sheets. His fever had broken during the night. The sun was shining hot through the window; the air was thick, his nose still stuffed. He stared out the window and debated with himself whether to jump and

82

make a run for it before the others awakened. Before he could make up his mind, there was a knock at the door.

"May I come in?" It was Deborah, coming to check on him. "Are you decent?"

"Come in," he replied.

"I brought you a change of clothing," she said. "You're about the same size as Ashel. He was kind enough to lend these to you till yours are washed and dried."

"Ashel?"

"Yes, he's one of the other guests staying here. How are you feeling? Any better today?"

"A lot better," he replied. "Good enough that I was thinking about moving on."

"You should wait at least till after you've eaten breakfast," she replied, silently thinking to herself that it would be better for all concerned if he left.

Harry was hungry, and he didn't have much money left. "Okay," he said. "If you're sure you don't mind?"

"No, I don't mind. How would you like to take a walk on the beach before we eat?"

"That would be great," he replied. "I've never seen the ocean before."

"You finish dressing. I'll wait downstairs for you."

***

"What are you doing out there? Come in." Hamish saw Deborah standing in the open door to the study. "What are you up to this hot, muggy morning?"

"Oh, nothing. I'm waiting for Harry to get dressed. I said I would take him for a walk on the beach before breakfast."

"Then I take it our mystery man is feeling better."

"Yes, it seems so."

A worried expression shadowed Deborah. "What's the matter with you guys?" She stared over at Ashel and his brother Al. "You both look like death warmed over."

"We just received some bad news," replied Ashel. He paused. "Isidor Steinberg has been shot down outside his Washington apartment."

"Oh no. My God!" Deborah's hand flew to her mouth. "Then our worst fears are true. The terrorists have struck!"

"It looks that way," sadly replied Hamish. "Isidor was an old and good friend of mine. We fought together in the War of Independence. Once he saved my life."

"Do the police have any idea who did it?" Deborah, wobbly on her feet, leaned up against the wall.

Ashel replied bitterly. "The police say they haven't a clue. I'm sure that they're not too interested in finding the killers of a Jewish lobbyist."

"An eye for an eye," said Al. "Yes. Why not? It's the only language the Arabs and the Communists understand. I hope we have the good fortune to have them try something here!"

Hamish caught Al's slip of the tongue right away and tried covering it up. "We have only so many people here in the States. There is a limit to how much we can do. We have orders to protect those we have identified as the most likely targets and are doing all we can to protect them."

"I see..." Deborah eyed her father suspiciously. She always could tell when he was trying to hide something from her. And when her father suggested that after breakfast she should take Harry back to New York, Deborah knew for sure that her father was up to something.

"What are you guys planning to do about the terrorists in the meantime?" she pried.

"Our best men and women," replied Ashel, "are at this very moment searching for the killers. We have the faint hope that we will find them before they attempt their next kill."

"We wait and pray," added Al.

"That's what I would like to know." She stared hard at Al.

"What...?" I don't get you?" He cocked his head.

Deborah replied that she was under the impression that he and Ashel were the best the Mossad had to field in North America.

"I don't like to sound our bell too often," replied Al. "But we like to think we're the best intelligence team working in all the world.

"Why?"

"Enough of this cat and mouse," interrupted Hamish. "I gather, gentlemen, that my daughter has already guessed what we're up to."

"I believe I have, and I can't say I like it one bit! You've set yourself up as bait, hoping that this will be the next place the Arabs strike. Right?"

"Right," replied Ashel. "We've laid a trail of crumbs from Jerusalem to here that even a stupid Arab couldn't miss."

"How?"

"There's this Jewish businessman who was planning to vacation here," replied Hamish. "We received information from a reliable source that he was on the Arab's list. The Arabs don't know me, so I took his identity and came here hoping they would follow."

"Why you?"

"Damn it all, girl!" The tension was there in Hamish's voice.

"It's my job. I couldn't ask anyone else to do my duty for me, could I?"

Deborah was about to protest when she saw Harry out of the corner of her eye, standing outside the study in the hallway.

"Hi," he said, not sure if he should come in the room or not. Self-conscious he was when he met strangers.

"Harry!" Hamish bounced out of his seat. "Come in, come in. We don't allow anyone to remain a stranger long in my family. I'd like you to meet a couple of friends of Deborah's and mine. Both good Jewish young men."

"Hi," greeted Ashel.

"Hi." Al shook Harry's hand. "Glad to meet you."

Deborah darted dirty looks at her father but took his hinting that he wanted her to take Harry out for his promised walk on the beach.

"You guys," she turned to the brothers, "want to take a walk on the beach with us?" She was reluctant to leave, but she had promised.

"No…" Ashel replied for both he and Al. "We have a few matters we want to talk over with your father." He gave her a you-know-what look.

Hamish stared after Deborah and Harry walking out of the house. "Spunk!" he said proudly. "Takes more after her mother every day, God rest her gentle soul."

"That is some fine woman you have for a daughter," agreed Ashel. "She does have a lot of energy."

"That's the kind of people Israel needs," added Al.

"What about him?" questioned Ashel. "What do you know about Harry?"

"I don't know much, to tell you the truth," Hamish replied. "I met him on the train down here. I know he's a Jew, and I have my suspicions that he's in some kind of trouble. I said that I would try and help him out, and I intend doing just that, for your information. If my daughter hasn't told you, I expect you guys to be nice to him. He's a bit jumpy."

"Take it easy yourself," replied Ashel. "Weren't we nice to him? My brother and I are nice to everyone if we can be. Aren't we, Al?"

"Yes, of course we are. But you have to understand that we have a job to do."

"What my brother means to say is that it is our responsibility to keep a suspicious eye on him. Our enemies have been known to recruit some of our own people to fight against us."

"Agreed," replied Hamish. "But discreetly. I don't want you two scaring him away. Is that understood?"

"Understood," the brothers replied in unison.

"By the way," said Ashel. "I didn't catch his last name."

"I don't believe he ever said," replied Hamish.

"Didn't you ask?"

"No, I haven't."

"You think it would be a good idea if we did?" Ashel held up the flat part of his hand. "Discreetly, of course. But I do believe it would be a good idea to have a check run on your friend."

"Yes, but ask nicely," Hamish smiled. "I'm not worried about him. He's probably one of the most harmless people I have ever met."

"Let's all hope so," replied Ashel.

— CHAPTER TEN —

"The ocean," exclaimed Deborah, standing in awe of its size, her hair blowing in the wind, a smattering of salt spray in her face. "Doesn't make any difference how many times I visit; she's inspiring, her magnificence."

Irritating Harry was the sand in his shoes. He kicked the beach. "It sure doesn't smell the way I imagined it would. Whh…! It stinks!"

"Have a little reverence for the dead fish washed in by the tide to their final resting place, rotting," replied Deborah. "In a few hours, the tide will roll out to sea, taking with her earthy fragrance. My mother used to say" —she dug her feet in the sand—that the ocean reminded her of the miracle of God. Spread out as far as the eye can see, waves playfully romp in on the beach, washing white water covering the sands, rolling back tide, changing the landscape. In all her glory! Oh Man!"

"Ohhh…" Harry could care less.

That annoyed Deborah, who was doing her best to be nice to him. An uneasiness pervaded their silence. 'I really don't believe this guy,' she thought to herself. 'He's weird! So what? It's no crime to be different.' She thought she would give him another go.

"I personally don't believe in all that religious stuff myself. If the religious fanatics had it their way, our enemies would wait for nightfall on Fridays to attack, and we'd invite them in for the Seder."

This time, Harry said nothing, not one word, not a grunt, nothing to show he was paying her the least bit of attention.

"Harry…?" She said, "Harry…?" Her tone was accusing. "Who are you? Oh, I mean, who are you? Where do you come from? What are you doing down at the Shore at this particular time?" She locked eyes on him.

Frightened! "I don't have to tell you anything if I don't want to. I'm leaving!"

"No, don't!" She quickly put her hand on his knee. "You don't have to tell me anything. You're right; that's your right. Not if you don't want to. But I would like to know."

He pouted.

What was there to say? She fiddled around, running her toes through the sand. It tickled.

"Try it," she suggested to Harry. "Take your shoes and socks off. It feels wonderful."

"Sure," he surprised her. "I'm used to having my feet in the sand. I sure got plenty in my boots in the army."

"What...?" She didn't quite understand.

"Yes, why not! In fact,"—he" puffed out his bony chest—"I "was in Special Forces. When everybody else was fighting in Nam, I was assigned as an advisor in Guatemala. I hunted Che for more than a year."

"You did? You ever catch him?"

"No. He was as slippery as an eel. All I got to show for my time is a bullet in the back. I also have a sixty percent disability."

"You were wounded?"

"That's what I said. Got me these pieces of sharp metal still in the base of my spine. The doctors at first believed that I'd never walk again. Had five operations, was in a cast from my ankles to my neck for more than eight months."

"But you're okay now?"

"It was a miracle," he bragged. "After the fifth operation, the surgeons said they could go back in for a sixth time, but the remaining fragments were lodged so close to my spine that there was a fifty-fifty chance they'd sever the spinal column. I took the hard way and told them to forget it. From there on, I was on my own. It was up to me to get off my ass or be confined to a wheelchair for the rest of my life."

"Harry." Deborah didn't know whether to believe him or not. "You're a brave man. Israel needs all the people like you she can get to come."

Out of the blue, for no apparent reason, Harry turned sour. "If you don't mind," he said queerly, "I think I would like to head back to the house now; I'm not feeling too good all of a sudden."

"What did I say?"

Deborah couldn't think of a thing. "All right, Harry. Breakfast is probably ready. We might as well start heading back."

Having nothing to say to each other as they walked back to the house, as a matter of habit, Deborah kept a cautious eye around her. Down the beach, a long way away, she saw a shadowy figure coming their way. An uneasy feeling crept up her back. She was almost trotting to keep up with Harry and could hardly not notice him nervously glancing over his shoulder. She began to have suspicions about her father's newfound friend.

"Someone you know?" asked Deborah.

"No," he replied. "I don't know anyone in these parts."

"You know us," she replied. She saw that whoever it was, was now sitting down towards the water's edge. "Some vacationer taking a morning walk, I guess."

"Ohh…?"

Within sight of the house, Harry surprised her. "You know, you're the prettiest girl I have ever known."

"Really!" Deborah laughed. "Now you have me saying it."

"What?"

"Really, silly."

"Don't laugh at me!" Harry got mad. "I don't like people making fun of me."

"I wasn't making fun of you. I think you're kinda cute."

"You're lying! You're like everybody else. They don't like me either."

"Hey?" Hamish, standing on the back porch, said. "What

are you two arguing about?"

"Oh, nothing, Dad," shrugged Deborah. "We were only talking." She excused herself gracefully, saying she'd like to wash up before breakfast.

"It wasn't my fault," Harry said as soon as Deborah disappeared into the house. "Maybe... I think it would be better if I left."

"If you think that's best, I wouldn't try and stop you," Hamish replied. "I promised you I wouldn't, but why don't you wait till you've had breakfast? I bet you're starved!"

"I am, but I'm afraid that your daughter doesn't like me too much."

"Don't worry about her. Take my word for it; I'm her father. She's a proud woman. It takes you a while to get used to Israeli women. They're not exactly like your typical girls here in America. More spunky, independent. It's the kind of life we're forced to live in Israel. Where everyone is strained by circumstances to do the so-called 'man's work.' Taking their equal share on and all that."

"She's not an American?" Harry had no idea he was with foreigners.

"Yes and no," he replied. "She went to work on a kibbutz a number of years ago and liked it so much that she stayed on. At this moment, she has dual citizenship."

"You let her?"

"Of course, I'm proud of Debbie."

"Oh, I see," said Harry, but actually he didn't see at all.

***

"What the hell is this all about?" Ashel stopped Deborah as soon as he saw her come in the house.

"What's what the hell about?" She flung around.

"Who the hell is that guy, anyways?" snapped Ashel.

"Why yell at me?" Deborah glared. "He's just a guy father picked up on the train. My father is a kind man. If he has any weaknesses, it's that sometimes he's too kind, but don't yell at me! I had nothing to do with Harry being here. You have a bitch! Take it to the Man!"

"I'm sorry," Ashel replied on reflection. "This whole business is beginning to get on my nerves."

"Don't be," tartly she replied. "Father is a bleeding heart. He picks up strays of all sorts—people, dogs, cats, you name it—if it's in need of help. Father is there with an open heart."

"And brought him here! Now! A stranger! That's not too smart if you ask me."

"Well, as far as I know, no one has," she turned her back, holding her head higher than usual, and walked away.

"Nothing wrong with that woman's spirit." Ashel liked Deborah very much.

***

Hamish's gaiety and good humor lifted the spirits of everyone at breakfast. Sitting at the head of the table, with Deborah on his right, Harry on his left, and Ashel and Al sitting across from each other.

The meal was composed of Harry's favorite food. He smacked his lips. He couldn't decide what to reach for first.

"Dig in," exclaimed Hamish, reaching for the dish of creamed herring.

He began with black bread and cream cheese, a dash of black pepper, a tomato cut into small pieces, and another dab of pepper. Next to his tomatoes, Harry piled high, in a neat mound, the creamed herring and onions. He cleaned a small white fish and asked Ashel if he would please pass the bagels and lox.

"Ahh..." Harry bit in. His cheeks were puffed with herring.

"You see," exclaimed Hamish. "A Jew can never lose his taste for real Jewish food. It's in the blood."

"Hmmm..." stuffed Harry, thoroughly enjoying himself.

"You're stuffing it in like you haven't eaten in some time." Ashel asked, not as friendly as he could have been.

"Whh…" Harry pretended he didn't hear him. He went on eating. "This sure is good!" he said to Hamish. "I believe you're right. Yes! Without a doubt! This is my favorite meal."

"I said," repeated Ashel, "that you're stuffing your mouth like there's no tomorrow."

"I'm probably not going to be fortunate enough to eat as good." He couldn't ignore him any longer.

"He's right, you know," Hamish came to his rescue. "You never know what you're putting in your stomach these days. Every day on the news, they're telling you another food is reported to cause cancer."

"And about everything else you can think of," added Deborah. "Jelly, toothpaste, baby powder, bacon, water, car fumes, cigarettes, baby formula, the very air we breathe. You name it; it causes cancer."

"Unless you grow it yourself," replied Harry. "You can never be sure it's safe unless you do."

"Did you know," Hamish said, "that Israel is the first nation in the Middle East to export food in over two thousand years?"

"No, I didn't," replied Harry. He choked on a bone slipping down the wrong pipe.

"You hear," said Al, "that the Bank of America was blown up in New York yesterday?"

Harry's heart thumped. He put his fork down, lowered his eyelids, and through a narrow slit scoped out the others, thinking they knew who he was and Al was trying to trick him into giving himself away. "Not me…"

"No," said Hamish. "I've been too busy the last couple of days to follow the news. What happened?" Hamish had an idea that maybe there was a connection between the bank bombing and the terrorist they were trying to smoke out.

"I only hear that there were four of them. The news reported that one of the bombers was identified by an eyewitness outside the bank."

"You hear anything about that, Harry?" asked Al. "You came from the city about the same time it happened."

"1 wouldn't know," his voice trembled, knees knocking. He forced another bite down but couldn't swallow it. He spit it in his napkin, rolled it up, and put it in his pocket. "I never watch television," he replied.

"Or read newspapers, or listen to the radio, I suppose," sarcastically said Ashel.

"If you ask me," Hamish stared coldly at Ashel, "it's a nice break to take a rest from the news once in a while. Isn't that right, Harry?"

"Hmm..." He was shaken by the mere mentioning of the bombing. He wanted to run, dig himself a hole, and never come out.

Relentlessly, Ashel bored in. "Say, Harry. Deborah tells me you're a vet."

"That's right."

"What branch?"

"I was in the army," he replied uneasily.

"What was it like?"

"What was what like?"

"Vietnam."

"I wasn't in Vietnam. I was stationed in Guatemala." A pained expression twisted his features. "If you don't mind, I'd rather not talk about my combat experiences."

"I see..." replied Ashel, shaking his head at his brother. "By the way, Harry, I never did catch your last name?"

"Me neither," said his brother. Everyone waited in silence for Harry to answer.

What was Harry going to do? He flushed white.

"Harry?" Hamish leaned across at him. "You haven't any reason not to tell us? Have you?"

"No," he stuttered, his head fizzling. "Megiddo!" He blurted, hoping that he slurred it enough and they would let it go at that.

"What?" Ashel cocked his head. "I didn't get it."

"Megiddo!" He felt cornered. "Harry Megiddo!" His voice cracking. He stared around at the others for a sign that they knew his secret. He swallowed. The saliva stuck in his throat. He coughed.

"Megiddo?" Hamish almost tumbled off his chair.

"Harry," gasped Deborah.

Harry saw the reaction his name caused. "They know!" He panicked, jumped to his feet, knocked his chair over, and ran for the door.

The others, momentarily startled, didn't move for a few seconds. "Go get him and bring him back," yelled Hamish.

Ashel nodded to his brother, who was up in a shot and out of the room in a flash.

***

Letting Ashel have her dirtiest, coldest, meanest "look— "Megiddo!"

Deborah was flabbergasted. "Naugh...? I don't even believe in God!" She tried making light of it, but no one laughed.

"You call what you did to Harry being discreet?" Hamish, beside himself, said to Ashel. He, too, was hiding his astonishment by getting mad at someone else.

"Now Hamish," replied Ashel. "I might have gotten carried away there for a second, but..."

"Look!" Hamish broke in. "If you and your brother can't follow orders, maybe you two ought to be doing something else! He didn't do anything to deserve the kind of third degree you guys put him through!"

"It's my job!" retorted Ashel. "You said so yourself! To do anything that is necessary to stop the murders of our people! Remember? We're on the same side."

"You can't be thinking that Harry's working for the Arabs?" Deborah, incredulous, blurted. "He's not bright enough."

"I don't know," he replied. "I don't know. He ran, didn't he?"

"He ain't running no more." They all turned towards the door.

There was Al, struggling to hold on to a kicking and scratching Harry.

"Let me go! Let me go!" Harry fought for all he was worth. "I didn't know what they were up to. I didn't! I swear to God! It wasn't my fault! You've got to believe me!" He ceased struggling and slumped in Al's grasp.

"Now what in the heck is this all about?" Ashel walked slowly over to him and lifted his slumped head by the ears.

"You know," cried Harry. "I swear to you that I didn't know what they were doing."

"No, we don't know! Tell us!" menaced Ashel.

Hamish grabbed Ashel by the wrists. "Let him go," he ordered. "I'm not kidding, Ashel! Let him go!"

Reluctantly, Ashel stepped back. His brother pushed Harry down in a chair.

"Don't try it!" He saw Harry glance at the window.

Deborah gave Harry a glass of water. "Drink this," she said kindly, pitying the poor fellow.

Hamish waited till Harry drank it all down. "You calmed down enough now to answer a few questions?"

"Yes," Harry wiped his eyes.

"The sooner you answer my questions, the sooner you'll be off the hot seat. Remember, I said I wanted to help you. I still do. You understand that?"

Sniveling, he nodded he understood.

"Why did you run?"

"You know."

"Know what, Harry?"

"Know that I took part in the bombing of that bank in

New York. You know, and you're going to turn me over to the police!"

Harry panicked and bolted for the window. Al was waiting for that move. Harry turned and ran for the door. Ashel blocked his way.

"I didn't mean to do it!" Harry jumped up and down. "I didn't know what they had planned. I tried to find out, but they wouldn't tell me. I didn't!" He screamed, but nothing came out.

Ashel and his brother circled in on him.

"We believe you." Hamish tried to calm him down. "Take it easy. We're all friends here. Believe me, no one is going to hurt you."

"No, you don't!" Harry's head frantically jerked from side to side. He bolted between the terrible brothers, breaking through their outstretched hands. He ran full tilt into the wall, bounced off, and crumbled to the floor.

"Out cold." Ashel knelt over him.

"You sure he isn't dead?" worriedly asked Hamish. "He ran into that wall without flinching as hard as he could. Almost as if he wanted to kill himself. Poor guy."

"He's breathing," replied Ashel. "Other than a cut on his forehead and a little blood dripping from his nose, I can't find anything broken. I believe your friend will survive."

Harry moaned.

"He's coming around." Ashel stopped feeling around.

"Al," ordered Hamish. "Help Debbie take Harry upstairs. You better stay with him and make sure that nothing else happens to our friend. I'll be up as soon as I can. I still have a few questions I want to put to him."

Harry, dazed, was helped to his feet and led from the room without a struggle.

Shaking off what had transpired, "My God!" exclaimed Hamish. "The implications are incredible! Almost mind-boggling!"

"What's the big deal?" shrugged Ashel. "Turn him over

to the cops, and we wash our hands of the whole matter."

"What's the big deal?" Hamish could barely contain himself. He was staggered.

"What's the problem? We have more important matters to think about. You haven't forgotten the terrorists?"

"Don't be stupid!" Hamish tapped his fingers. "That's all we need. Turn Harry in. Get his name in the papers, plastered all over the country. It wouldn't be five minutes before some hot-shot reporter ties our Harry Megiddo in with the Messiah that lunatic has been preaching about all these years back home. Har Megiddo!"

"I still don't get it. You're not telling me that you believe for one second that Harry is the Messiah?"

"It doesn't make any difference what you or I believe. Whether Harry is or isn't is not the point. If people believe, then to them it's true. Our enemies within and without could make trouble for all of us out of this simpleton Megiddo. I can see the headlines now! Harry Megiddo, murderer, terrorist, Jewish menace, or Messiah?"

"What do you plan on doing with him then?"

"I plan to move cautiously. He mustn't be allowed out of our sight until we can get a message through to Jerusalem and see what they think. Take my word for it. This situation is going to have to be handled delicately, or there could be big trouble. Big trouble!"

— CHAPTER ELEVEN —

Yeshaayia Gurevich loved the desert. Where others saw an expanse of nothing out there, hot and inhospitable, he saw a land dripping with honey, gardens of flowers, groves of fruit, the Messiah, Har Megiddo, urging the people onward and 'up, heaven here on earth.

"Crazy old man! Lunatic!" They jeered at him. "Out of our way!" They pushed him aside, easing onto his shoulders the burden of every day in a nation at war since its creation. Anyway, that was what he chose to believe. He did not see what they were doing. He could no longer hear any of their jeers. He was too busy searching each and every face for the Spirit of the Lord. What he saw were poets and philosophers, artisans, and lovers strolling in the early evening.

Mistaking a date tree for a friend, Yeshaayia asked if he had seen Har Megiddo.

The date tree dropped a fruit at his feet.

"Oh, what a magnificent day!" Yeshaayia danced off on his tiptoes, convinced that he was close to finding the Messiah.

Meanwhile, Rabbi Tzadikovich was beginning his second week of imprisonment and accompanying fasting. His physical condition had been reported to be deteriorating. His old heart could not take the strain much longer. The worst was feared, and the government still refused to give in to his demands.

Outside the jail, the Guardians of Jerusalem were staging a not-so-peaceful vigil. Only a few hours earlier, the followers of Rabbi Tzadikovich mistook a curious onlooker for the Prophet Yeshaayia and almost beat him to death before the police arrived without a second to spare to save the innocent's life. A half dozen of the faithful were arrested and charged with aggravated assault. The victim was listed in a critical condition.

"We don't hold out much hope for him," a spokesman for the hospital announced. "The patient arrived in a coma, massive internal bleeding, half his head caved in. We're doing all that is humanly possible. Believe me!" He asked the family of the patient to have pity on the hospital personnel.

A short distance away, at the Wazo Youth Center, a suicide mission from the Black September Movement blew themselves to smithereens, along with thirteen Jewish children. Exactly three hours later, the Israelis responded with a vengeance. Officials at the Palestinian Camp claimed that three children, three old women, and three old men were killed along with the destruction of more than a third of all buildings in the camp. Momentarily, all over Israel, the police readied a massive round-up of all suspected Arab sympathizers. Later, a hundred and thirty-three people were arrested without being charged under the Emergency War Powers Act. Yeshaayia's head filled with people in the morning and emptied in the evening. But still no sign of the Savior.

***

Harry, shut up in the guest room, paced back and forth, twisting his hands, kicked the furniture, and fell flat on the bed. Or else he remained without eating, staring out the window down at the beach below. He was broken-hearted over what he had done. Sometimes, he squeezed his eyes till he saw stars, whining at the days that had passed, thinking there's no such thing as tomorrow because when tomorrow gets here, it's today.

"God! Sometimes...! Sometimes... it's damn hard to face another one."

Later that same day, Hamish was keeping Harry company. "You have to be kidding," frowned Hamish. "On top of everything else..." He twisted the ends of his hair round his pinky. He didn't know what to believe.

"You mean to tell me that you never once smiled in your whole life?"

"Never once," Harry replied. "You ever see me?"

"No!"

"The way I grew up, there wasn't ever anything to smile

about. I was one of the middlings of eleven children. My grandma lived with us in Brooklyn. When there's that many people living under the same roof, there's just so much love and affection that parents can spread about. Somehow, I always seemed to get lost in the crowd."

"I always thought that big families were close. Friends…!"

"I once remember," Harry pushed his lips out with the tip of his tongue, "I was nine years old and out in the alley behind our apartment building when I stumbled over my oldest brother, lying face down between two trash cans. Later, I learned he was dead! Killed himself, or maybe someone else did it for him from an overdose of heroin."

"My gosh!"

"Yes, and that wasn't all I went through. I was always afraid to go to school because the other kids were always beating me up. Catching me on the way to or from, maybe in the playground."

"Incredible!"

"After I graduated from high school, I went into the army. You know, from the day I arrived at the reception center till the day I mustered out… If I didn't have bad luck, I wouldn't have any luck at all. And that's the truth!"

"I believe you, Harry. How can I make you believe me? My only wish is to help you."

The sun was going home for the night, having had enough. He was disgusted. Here comes the moon out for a stroll. A cool breeze ever so gently rocked the leaves of the trees. Rock-a-bye baby. Hamish set Harry at ease. He had a purpose in mind.

"Harry?"

"Yeh."

"How would you like to go to Israel?"

"I don't know," he replied. "I don't know what I should do."

"We are your friends, Harry! We want what's best for

you. In Israel, you'll be safe among your own kind. No more looking over your shoulder for the bogeyman. You'll be among friends who will protect you."

"My own people," Harry muttered under cover of slurring his words together, thinking that he didn't have any more reason to trust the Jews than he had to trust anyone else.

"You have any money?" Hamish questioned.

"Not much."

"You have any friends that you can ask for help?"

"No, no one."

"What about your family? Would they be willing to stick their necks out?"

"They can't. They're too poor to help themselves, never mind me. No..." he fretted, wishing Hamish would get off his back. "I'm on my own."

"Then what choice do you have? We want to be your friends. I want to help you. No strings attached. What do you say?"

Harry pouted. "That's what everyone says. Then! Bam! I get it every time, right in the old kisser."

***

"Damn it!" uptightly yelled Ashel. "What's keeping them?"

"My brother's right! Hey man, this place could turn into a free-for-all anytime. I say, let's get the jerk out of here to a place of safety. Then, we can wait to hear from Jerusalem without worrying about the Arabs and Harry at the same time."

Hamish scratched the back of his hand. "Let's give our people a little more time. If we don't hear from them, say, in one hour, I'll send Deborah back to the city with Harry."

"Do we have a choice?" replied Al. "You're the man, like you said to my brother. You give the orders. We're here to obey, not advise."

"That's right," easily replied Hamish. "Why don't you

cool off outside, and while you're at it, you might as well have a good look around." He smiled.

Al looked to Ashel for approval.

"Go ahead," he replied. "Be careful! I don't like the feel of things." He turned and faced Hamish.

"Ahh…" he flicked his hand in the air. "What could happen in an hour? We knew when we set this deal up that it was a one-in-a-million shot. I'm kind of happy that the Arabs passed or missed us. Too many imponderables going on."

"I hope you're right," replied Hamish, thoughtfully. "But I don't know. We better keep on our toes. I have this gnawing feeling in my gut that I'm overlooking something obvious."

"Know what you mean," he replied. "I've had a similar feeling ever since you brought that guy into the house. If there was ever a more unlikely candidate for a Messiah, I couldn't imagine one."

***

Out of sight, a mile offshore, an oil freighter, flying the Liberian flag, dropped anchor. The house was quiet, eerily so. The wind blowing off the ocean pushed against the windowpanes, creaking. The sky was hidden behind a thick layer of cumulus clouds; heavy air oppressively pressed down on the snobby little seaside resort. Sweating clean through his shirt, Harry reeked so badly that Deborah was forced to breathe through her mouth.

"If you care to get it off your chest," she offered, "I'd be more than happy to lend you an ear."

"The worst part about being there was the loneliness."

"You ever killed anyone?" Deborah didn't know what to believe, but she asked anyway.

"If I had to," he replied. "Once, we assaulted this village at the foothills of the mountains. The rebels split into the jungle as we headed in. We found a bunch of friendlies. There were six of them, bound hand and foot to short stakes. Their eyes had been burned out, their fingernails ripped back to the wrists, and

103

the skin on their chests had been tortuously peeled back to the bone. None of 'em weighed more than a sack of potatoes. They begged us to end their miseries. I still hear them screaming sometimes during the night, and that was more than ten years ago. It was terrible! So, I did the only thing that a decent person could do under the circumstances. I shot four of 'em before I started puking over myself. Someone else, I don't know who, shot the rest."

"I'm not sure what to say." Deborah was totally at a loss for words, maybe for the first time in her life.

"Yes, and I did a lot of drugs while I was in Guatemala. You know, I read somewhere that Guatemala was the first of the psychedelic wars. The others, like World War One and Two and Korea, were fought high on alcohol. Even in Nam, I read that the Guatemala vets turned the G.I.'s on in Nam. In all the time I fought in South America, I never met anyone who didn't smoke marijuana."

"No kidding?"

"And you know what else?"

"No? What?" She pretended she was on every word he was saying. Even if what he said was true, and she had her doubts, who cared!

"I bought this girl from her father for twenty-five dollars and a dime a day for her. For an extra dime, you could get her to bounce around on a pogo stick stuck up her you-know-what."

Deborah bit her tongue. "He's full of it," she thought to herself. "And dumb as hell..."

"I wasn't like that, of course," Harry swelled out his chest. "But some of the other guys in my outfit had some pretty perverted tastes, you know."

"I know, I know," she replied. "Some men are like that. I'm glad you're a different sort of person. You'll like the women in Israel." She smirked to herself: 'the question is whether they can stomach him!'

"Me too . . . "

104

"I bet you've made love to plenty of women in your time."

"I'm nothing great," he smugly replied. "But I do have to admit to you that I've had more than my fair share."

"I bet!"

"I remember this one time," Harry barely paused to catch a breath. "It was in the beginning of one summer vacation. I was up on the New England coast working as a bartender."

"Hmm...?" Deborah remembered he said he had never seen the ocean before this morning.

"I arrived late and couldn't find a room to stay in, and one of the girls who was working in the same joint as a waitress offered me a place to sleep for the night."

"That was nice of her." Deborah swallowed a yawn.

"Sure was!" Harry didn't hear the note of sarcasm in her voice. "Anyways, after work I went home with her. Her roommate greeted me like I was a long-lost lover. I think now, remembering back, that she took to me right off."

"Wouldn't surprise me a bit."

"They had a one-room efficiency apartment with a double bed in the middle of the room and a fold-out cot in the corner; that's where I was to sleep, they said."

"So we all went to bed. I slipped off my clothes in the light shining through the single window. I have to admit that I was a little embarrassed undressing in front of two strange girls."

"That's understandable," replied Deborah. "I would have felt the same myself."

She thought to herself that he is a clutz. "What happened next?"

She glanced impatiently at her wristwatch and wondered what everyone else was doing. She couldn't leave. Her father had ordered her to stay put till she was relieved. She came back into what Harry was saying. Who knew how long he had been going on? "They got into bed and switched this blue light on. The night was quiet, and I was restless my first night in a strange town. I kept hearing these strange noises, giggling and soft whispering. My eyes adjusted, and I stared over to where they were sleeping. Unbelievable! I couldn't believe my eyes. You know what they were doing?"

"Making love," nonchalantly replied Deborah.

"How...? How'd you know?" surprised Harry."

"A lucky guess. What happened next?"

"One thing led to the next, you know what I mean..."

"You got turned on."

"Right!" Blushed Harry. "I still can't remember coming over to their bed, but there I was standing over them, peering down. The girl that brought me home looked up. Her eyes were flaming with need; she begged me to join in; she grabbed my leg and pulled."

"So, what was the use in fighting!" Deborah laughed.

"Exactly!" Bragged Harry. "Tell you one thing, since that night, my love life hasn't been the same. The rest of the summer, say, I brought some ten other girls up to our little cozy nook. We'd get to bed, and after a few preliminaries, my roommates would show up, get undressed, and start making it. Well, let me tell you. Eight of the ten girls I brought up there ran for their lives. But the two that stayed...!" He took a deep breath and let the air out slowly. He whistled, "Sure had themselves one terrific good old time, they'll never forget!"

"Harry, you're magnificent!" exclaimed Deborah. "I never met anyone who has done as much as you have in so short a time."

"Thank you! Thank you!" Harry took a bow. "I have to admit that I've done as much as anyone I have ever met."

"Your modesty and openness overwhelm me," she replied.

"What else have you done?"

"Plenty," he quickly replied. "I graduated at the top of my class from college. I got to go out with the University Queen."

"Hey, that's terrific. I didn't know that you're bi-sexual?"

"What?" he stammered. "I am not!"

"Take it easy," Deborah castigated herself. She should have known by this time not to make jokes at his expense. "I was joking, Harry! Didn't mean anything by it! Come on, Harry! Don't start pouting on me again."

Harry turned away. He sat down on the bed heavily. No matter how Deborah pleaded, she said she was sorry and didn't mean anything by it.

"Please!" Harry refused to listen.

"Alright. Have it your own way." She opened the bedroom door.

"You sit tight. Don't try anything funny. I'll be right outside if you need me for anything." She shook her head. "I'll be right back." Closing the door behind her, she quickly made her way down the long hallway.

There, to her surprise, sitting at the top of the stairs was Ashel, his elbows on his knees, resting his head in his hands. He heard her coming and looked up.

"Hi! How's the Messiah?" he forced a grin.

"He's pouting again," she replied, sitting down on the step. "Have hear any word on what to do with him yet?"

"No, and I'm getting worried. My brother and I tried talking your father into getting you and Harry out of here, but he, as you know, is a stubborn man."

"I know, I know. He can be a mule sometimes. I was just thinking to myself that I can hardly believe all this is happening. I'd say it's a bit strange! Wouldn't you say?"

"It seems my brother and I have been in this business for a hundred years, and nothing surprises us any longer."

"You hear something?" Deborah squeezed Ashel's hand. Something was wrong, not quite right. She had a feeling and stared intently down the stairs, her senses alive for any sign of trouble. There was none in sight.

"I guess I'm a little jumpy," she said after a few more

107

seconds of careful listening.

"Been spending too much time with the Messiah," replied Ashel. "He's as uptight as anyone I've ever had the displeasure of meeting."

"Boy is he ever," she replied with a nervous laugh. "And it's contagious. Look at me!"

She held out a trembling hand. "I've been more steady under…"

She didn't have a chance to finish.

A shot rang out, freezing her tongue in mid-sentence. Then another and another.

"Al!" Ashel hollered, and before her tongue unfroze, he was bounding down the steps by threes, his gun in hand.

Another shot rang out as Ashel disappeared. Then another. "Father!" Deborah shouted, taking a couple of steps down before she remembered Harry.

Turning, she ran back up, with no thought of her own safety, down the hallway. She flung open the door to the guest room.

Another shot rang out!

Harry was standing at the window.

"What's that?" He turned as soon as he heard her come in.

"Get down!" She hollered and flung herself on him, knocking them both down on the floor.

"What'd you do that for?" Harry tried getting up.

"Get down," she restrained him. You damn fool. You want to get yourself killed!"

"Killed!" whirled in Harry's mind.

"Stay low." Deborah pulled Harry along the floor. "Stay low and follow me closely." Her voice trembled.

If Deborah had had the time to look behind her, she would have seen Harry wetting his pants, dripping down his pants legs and leaving a trail as he crawled.

Out of the bedroom and back down the hallway, she led Harry crawling on all fours, ever so slowly, carefully avoiding trouble.

"Oh my God, oh Mighty," swore Harry. "Not again! Why me? Goddamn it!"

"Shut up," hissed Deborah, glancing back. She saw his wet pants, him shaking like a leaf. "Pull yourself together," shaking him.

Down the stairs they crept. If Deborah had a wish, she would have asked for three: one, that her father was safe; two, she had a gun in hand; and three, that Harry would disappear never to be seen again by her.

At the bottom of the stairs, she got upon her feet, pulling Harry with her. "Oh..." she prayed. "Let my father be safe."

Suddenly, the den door swung open, and as if in an answer to her prayers, there was Hamish, gun in hand.

"Hold it!" Hamish swept a quick glance around. "There might be others in the house." He saw Harry—a more cowardly man he had never set eyes on.

"Deborah, take Harry in the other room. I'm going to take a look around the house. And be careful!"

"Where are the brothers?" She said as he brushed by.

"They're in there," he pointed. "Ashel's been hurt!"

"No!" she gasped. She pushed Harry into the library. There, lying on the floor with Al hovering over him, was Ashel's body, riddled with bullet holes, blood splattered all over the white carpet.

Across the room, lying in pools of their own blood, were two other men.

"Is he dead?"

Deborah checked the other men for any sign of life.

"No," replied Al, barely able to get the words out of his mouth. He loved his brother more than anyone else in the world. More than himself. Tears filled his eyes.

109

Surrounded by blood-stained carpet, furniture, and walls, "Somebody do something!" Harry was hysterical. "Do something!" He jumped up and down. "For God's sakes!" He covered his eyes.

"I'll call an ambulance," Deborah said as soon as she was satisfied that the other men were dead.

"No!" Al said shortly. "There's nothing more anyone can do for my brother." He held him in his arms and rocked him back and forth.

"Aren't you going to call a doctor!" Incredulously, screamed Harry. "What kind of people are you, anyways? My God, this is a massacre! I'm getting out of here!" He bolted for the door.

"Oh no you don't!" Hamish blocked his way. "Oh no you don't! You're not going anywhere!" He pushed him back.

"You have no right to keep me here against my will," stammered Harry. "It's against the law! I'm an American citizen!"

"Shut up!" Yelled Hamish, in no mood for one of Harry's tantrums.

"Get hold of yourself!" He shook him.

"Noo...!" He fought.

Hamish smacked Harry across the face with the back of his hand. His head snapped back. He groped for what was behind the thunder.

"You hurt me," Harry whined, rubbing his cheek.

"Your feelings are hurt more than your face," glared Hamish. "Now get over there!" He pointed to a chair in the middle of the room. "And keep your mouth shut!" In a way, Hamish felt sorry for him, but he didn't have the time now for sympathy.

Harry thought quickly about protesting but decided to do as he was told. His pants were wet. He backed towards where he was told to sit, afraid that the others would see him for what he was—a coward.

110

"We have to do something." Deborah gawked at poor Ashel. His body was riddled with bullet holes. Two in his chest had blown half his back out—one in his head, the crown dangling by a thread. It was a miracle he still was breathing.

"We have to chance it," sniffled Deborah.

"We can't," replied Hamish, feeling helpless. "If we could, we would, but you know as well as I that we can't". Ashel would understand, he hoped.

Al placed his hand on his brother's heart; his lips brushed his. "Too late," he said, barely audibly, grunting. "Too late, he's dead…!"

Hamish regarded what had happened. He was unable to tear his eyes off Al. He laid his hand on his shoulder, spreading over the whole of his face a sorrow deep and pitiful.

"Get that blanket," Hamish turned to Harry. "Over there," he ordered sternly. "There, on the couch."

"Put it over him."

"Do it! Damn you…!" cried Al.

Harry covered the mutilated body. He spread the blanket neatly, then jumped back, afraid that if he touched Ashel, his fate would rub off on him.

"Now what do we do?" Deborah said quietly.

Hamish wiped his hands. "We better be getting out of here as soon as possible. I'm sure one of the neighbors must have heard the shots. In any case, we can't take the chance of getting caught here by the police."

"Hey listen," said Harry, coming over to Al. "Why don't you just leave me here? I'm nothing but trouble to you people. If you do, I promise, I swear, I won't tell anyone what happened here today."

"You bet you won't!" Al grabbed Harry by the scruff of the neck and jerked his head down to his level. "You know why?" he screamed.

"No…" Harry cried.

"Because you ain't going nowhere without me! You hear?"

— CHAPTER TWELVE —

Seagulls dead and dying on the beaches, lying in the black gold washed up during the night. Rotting dead carcasses stinking to the high heavens met the sun worshippers who came early to the beaches.

Harry pulled the slipcover off the couch and laid it over one of the Arab terrorists. He was about to cover the other...

"What are you doing?" severely barked Al. "Don't bother!" His eyes were wild; he burned on a short fuse.

"Al's right," agreed Hamish. "It won't make any difference to them anyways. We aren't going to be here long enough for the sight of them to bother us. I see the sun's up already. We better be leaving while the getting is still possible."

Al grabbed Harry by the arm. "Do you hear? Do you hear? Look!" He forced Harry down to his knees and pushed his face into his brother's killer's uncovered open wounds.

"I didn't do anything!" Harry struggled to keep his head out of the bloody mess.

"I didn't do anything!" Al flung his revenge. "Is that any way for the Messiah to talk? 'I didn't do nothing!' " You didn't! You want the police to find you here? You want me to leave you here with a note nailed to your forehead telling them that you're one of the murderers that blew that bank up in New York? Hey! Hey!" He pushed down on Harry till his nose disappeared into the terrorist's guts. "I heard on the radio that one of the customers in the bank got killed." He let Harry up for air. He was all white.

"The woman was more than eight months pregnant! I bet there are a whole lot of angry people who'd like nothing better than to get their grimy hands on you!"

It was all too much for Deborah. Her better senses deserted her and took off for parts unknown. Enraged, she rushed at Harry, clawing his face, raking his skin under her fingernails.

"That's enough!" Hamish rushed over and dragged his daughter and Al off him.

"Why don't you fight back?" Deborah screamed. "Fight back, you coward!" Harry's mouth hung open.

"Hold it." Hamish struggled to keep control over the situation.

"You shut your mouth, or I might take Al's advice and leave you here for the police to find. Okay, okay," Hamish heaved. "We haven't got all the time in the world. We're all going to have to compose ourselves. "Debbie," he said, "get the car and pull it up the driveway."

"Why?"

"We can't very well leave Ashel here for strangers to bury in Potter's cemetery, can we?"

Al forced a smile. "Thanks," he said in anguished tones.

"Al, go out on the front porch and keep an eye out for trouble."

"You help me." He told Harry to get hold of Ashel's feet. "Now be gentle with him and don't drop your end. We'll put him in the trunk."

Harry gulped.

***

Across the street, Mrs. Boorum was sipping a glass of tomato juice and vodka, staring out her living room window. Yesterday she had seen her new neighbor. He was a handsome devil.

Deborah came out of the house.

"Must be his daughter..." She watched.

Deborah backed the car into the driveway, got out, and opened the trunk. As soon as she did, Hamish and Harry came out of the house carrying what Mrs. Boorum took to be a rug.

"Nice children, helping their dad keep the summer house up."

They lowered Ashel gently down, talked for a few

minutes, and went back into the house.

"Maybe I should visit the new neighbors. Bring them some flowers or something." She decided she would get out of her housecoat and into something light and summery.

A half-hour later, she was knocking at the front door.

No one answered.

She knocked again, pushing the door far enough open to see in.

"Hello," she hollered. "Hello..." she said louder. And when no reply came forthwith, "Hello...?" She then opened the door all the way and stepped in.

"God!" she exclaimed. The house was a wreck. She couldn't resist taking a look around.

Papers and sundry items scattered about, closets and drawers pulled open, clothes tossed on the floor. Her guess was that those people she had taken for granted who lived here were actually clever thieves robbing the house.

She searched for a phone. She was sure there'd be one in there and headed into the library to call the police.

"Oh my God!" Her eyes bulged wide in terror. Her heart thundered. She saw two men lying in a pool of dried blood, caked hard and fast over them. She screamed, felt dizzy, leaned back to catch her balance on the wall, and stuck her hand in a smear of blood. She shook furiously, only to splatter her nice yellow dress.

"Murder!" She turned pale and fled from the house, screaming and yelling for someone to help her. Terrified!

All over the neighborhood, her screams sounded loud and clear. She ran to the next-door neighbors and banged on the door. No answer. She fled to the next house down. The results were the same. As she was leaving, she saw peering at her through the window a face she recognized from downtown shopping. The curtains yanked shut!

She ran home and fell into a state of shock.

Late that evening, her husband returned home from a

very long day in the city and found his wife locked in the bathroom.

He banged on the door. "Let me in. I have to go to the bathroom." He figured she was in another one of her drunken stupors.

It took Mr. Boorum quite some time before he convinced his wife it was really him.

When she did, crying uncontrollably, she related hysterically what she had seen.

He called the police immediately.

They arrived at the scene soon after.

***

Hamish banged the phone down. This business was not to his liking, but it had to be seen through.

"And…" Al asked impatiently as Hamish came out of the phone booth.

"Good news and bad." He juggled his hands. "Let's get moving. I'll tell you on the way to the car."

Deborah and Harry had nothing to say to each other while they were waiting for the others to return. Harry's mind simmered; he hung unknowingly to him on the mercy of fate. Burned bridges washed into the stream in his wake. A shadow of guilt blocked his retreat; he knew he could never turn back now. And out in front of him, his fate danced a jig, eerie and heavy, compelling him to follow after into an unravelling universe. A din arose. He reflected it was better this way. He could no longer lose his way. His head cooled, his senses returned, his thoughts cleared, and when Hamish and Al returned, they found him tranquilly staring out the car window. Al gawked at Harry suspiciously, shrugged his shoulders, and dug his feelings clearly into the memory of his brother.

"What's up?" Deborah turned the engine over. "Where do we go from here?" She pulled away from the curve,

"First we go to bury Ashel," replied Hamish. "It's been arranged. Head out to the interstate, towards Long Island." He closed his eyes and grimaced.

***

The early evening found Harry in Beth David Cemetery digging a grave for Ashel. He wiped the sweat from his forehead. He wished he had a hat on his head, the brim keeping the flies out of his eyes. His hands were smooth and soon red and sore. Blisters broke through the air, split, and oozed. For as far as the naked eye could traverse, the cemetery spread out in front of him. Stone marker after stone marker interrupted by an occasional mausoleum poking its stone nose impudently up in the air. An hour passed quickly for Harry, working too slowly for the others watching from the air-conditioned car.

"Don't you think we ought to help him?" Deborah was still feeling guilty about raking Harry's cheek. "He looks like he's about ready to pass out!"

"Let him," thundered Al. "Who cares!" The smell of his brother's already decomposing body maddened his temper.

"We are in a hurry," Hamish said, turning up the air. The stink was making him sick.

"Let the Messiah finish digging my brother's grave himself. If it wasn't for him, Ashel might still be here with me now. We have the time! We make the time! We owe it to Ashel!"

Harry dug deeper and deeper. "Finally!" He threw the shovel to one side. "Finished!" He tried closing his hand but couldn't because of the swelling. Covered from head to foot with dirt, huffing and puffing, he tactlessly tapped on the car window in front of Al. "I got the hole dug," he said loudly.

Al rolled down the window, not hiding the contempt he felt for Harry. "Just like you told me to do. I hope it's big enough for your brother," said Harry. Without any warning, Al flung the car door open, hitting Harry in the shins as hard as he could.

"Ouch..." Harry fell back, reaching to rub his leg. "Why'd you do that?" sheepishly said he. "I didn't do nothing to you! I dug the hole! Why?"

"You're the Messiah," retorted Al. It felt good to be cruel

to Harry. He kicked some dirt on him. "You're not supposed to feel pain like the rest of us!" He chuckled at Harry's discomfort. "You're the Messiah!"

"Why are you always calling me dirty names?" Harry thought that Messiahs were only for Christians. He remembered when he was a kid and the other boys chased him, calling him the 'Christ-Killer!'

"Stop your whining, God damn you!" hollered Al. "I've about had enough of your belly-aching!"

"Easy does it!" Deborah took Al by the arm. "He's not worth your aggravating yourself over." She walked him over to the empty grave.

"Give me a hand!" Hamish opened the trunk.

"Can't it wait a few minutes?" replied Harry. "Man…, I'm dog tired."

"I have only you to help me, and I can't lift Ashel by myself. Don't make such a big deal out of everything, and people would take to you more."

"One…" "Two…"

"Three…"

"Lift...!" Hamish strained to lift his end up.

"Why is Al always calling me a Messiah?" Harry held Ashel insecurely by the armpits.

"Because, by coincidence, you have the same name as this guy in Israel who some say is the Messiah." Hamish tottered and changed his grip, bouncing the corpse off his knee.

"Oh, I see," replied Harry, his end sagging.

"Come on, Harry!" Hamish was breathing hard. "I can't hold him up by myself."

"Boy, is he ever heavy," panted Harry.

"Stop your belly-aching!"

"I'm no Messiah." Harry stumbled over his own feet and tumbled into the open grave. Ashel came falling in on top of him.

"Hey!" he cried, struggling to push the dead body to one

side. "Maybe?" Harry heard Al say madly that if he didn't get out, he'd bury him alive!

"Noo...!" Harry thought him serious. He shrieked, and with one mighty effort, he tossed the body up, slipped from under, stepped on Ashel's chest, propelling himself up and out of the hole.

He was met by a sharp slap in the face that knocked him flat.

Standing over him in a rage was Al. "You're damn lucky, damn lucky!" He shook a furious finger at him. "You're God damn lucky that I have my orders to bring you back to Israel alive. My brother gave his life for you. Heaven knows why. He's dead and you are not, but I warn you, if you give me the littlest excuse and make trouble, I swear I'll cut your throat!"

Harry groveled.

Al kicked the shovel lying at his feet towards Harry. "Go on," he menaced with obvious pleasure. "Fill it up!"

Oh God, did his body hurt! He prayed that after he had filled the grave, they'd let him go free. He pitied himself. His feelings were hurt as much as anything else. "Why me?" He repeated for the umpteenth time to himself. "Why is it always me who gets pushed around? Why can't one of the others get picked on for a change? My God, what have I done to deserve the honor always? Why can't I be like everyone else?"

He shoveled one last shovelful on, patting the dirt hard and smooth.

He laid the sod back on carefully. "There! No one will ever be able to tell that anyone's buried here. I'm done!" Dead tired on his feet, he wished he was dead.

The funeral was subdued and quickly over. Deborah stifled her tears and stood tall and straight, her eyes downcast.

"I'm sorry," she tried consoling, "that your brother isn't having a proper funeral." She bent low and placed a few stones on the sod, where she guessed the head was, then turned and walked slowly, dejectedly away.

A few more minutes passed in uneasy silence.

"Maybe," said Hamish, "later, when all this has passed, we can come back and get Ashel and take him home for a proper funeral."

"Maybe?" Al forced a smile.

"We have to be leaving," said Hamish, placing a hand on Al's shoulder. "I'm sorry, but it's not safe for us to stay here any longer. I see others arriving. We can't be found here. I have arranged for us to stay with this family, who are long-standing good friends of Israel, until the arrangements are completed to sneak us out of the country."

"That will be nice," sighed Al, who allowed Hamish to lead him away.

— CHAPTER THIRTEEN —

Harry Megiddo! Har Megiddo! Picked up by the wire services and broadcast round the world. In the United States, from one coast to another, the people talked about nothing else but Har Megiddo. Bank robber, murderer, Israeli agent, Messiah. There were tee shirts with a dozen different images of his likeness, hats and pillowcases, movies, and books coming out about him. Front page of all the big city daily's, front covers of Newsweek and Time. Every investigative reporter, available policeman, and citizen at their leisure entered into the new American craze of searching for the Messiah.

***

Far away in Jerusalem, Rachel, the daughter of Yeshaayia, shut up in her apartment, paced back and forth twiddling her fingers, or else she sat by the window wringing her hands, keeping an eye on the street below, waiting, waiting for the Rabbi to come and let her out of her prison. She had let her apartment go to hell. The dishes lay piled high on the drain board; cockroaches feasted magnificently on the garbage; the floors had not been swept; the dust thickly covered the furniture; the beds were unmade; and a stinking, musky odor permeated the place. She wore the same dress she had worn earlier after seeing her father. Her stockings clung to her ankles, her hair was dirty and sticky, and her eyes were sunken, tired, and red.

"And you smell from not bathing," Mordecai sulked into the apartment.

"You're driving my customers away." He started right in on her. "If you don't care about your appearance, the least you could do is stay away from the windows so that no one can see you. Look at this place," he disgustedly threw up his hands. "It's a pigsty in here! I can't go on living like this much longer!" He hollered, "I'm going out, and I don't know when I'm going to come back."

Rachel shrugged, more glad than sad that he was leaving

her alone. The narrow street of the quarter, as she stared, was empty. It was the Sabbath, the seventh day of the week, when God, along with man, rested from the toil of their labors.

At this very moment, the tall temple doors opened, and the faithful stumbled out, holding on to each other to regain their equilibrium. The sacred air of the old quarter echoed with excitement.

"The Hebrews are always excited about one thing or another," blase Rachel said to herself. "Each day brings its troubles." She had learned to live with terrorist bombings, demonstrations, and bullying Rabbi's, and nowadays she hardly cared.

As soon as she saw the people coming her way, she turned away from the window.

"Hey Rachel," she heard someone calling her from down on the street. She turned back. It was Nadab, the butcher.

"It's the Messiah!" He hollered, full of excitement. "The Messiah, he's coming! It's true!" He beamed up at her.

"You're joking…?"

"No! The years that your father prophesied have come. Everyone's heading out to the desert to see him."

She scoffed, "You and anybody else who believes my father's drunken rantings are as crazy as he is! Out of your minds!"

"No…!" shouted back Nadab. "Ask anyone! Go talk to your neighbors, turn on the radio or television, or buy a newspaper. You will see Har Megiddo. He's in America. Our people are trying now to rescue him and bring him home to us."

"And Rabbi Tzadikovich? What does he have to say about all of this?"

"Who cares what the fat Rabbi thinks! Let him starve to death, for all I care. He's coming! Har Megiddo comes!" Nadab danced down the street, hopping up and down, spreading the good news to all who would listen, and those who would not, he forced them to open their ears.

"Is it God who speaks through my father's mouth?" Rachel couldn't believe what she had always had the gnawing feeling was true. But she had never yet known the butcher to spread a false rumor.

And "listen—"Rachel!" A crowd of people had gathered under her window. Their numbers were ever increasing.

"Rachel!" they hollered, these God-fearing neighbors. "Where is your father? Rachel, come down and lead us to him." They shouted and wouldn't take her silence as an answer. They persisted, "Rachel! Take us to the Prophet!" They sung praises to the Messiah, Har Megiddo. Their savage song came out of Israel and beat at all the doors of the world.

***

In the Vatican, the Pope was the first who could not stand the Jews' singing. The lyrics gave him a splitting headache, leaving him no other choice but to denounce the people of Israel as lousy singers and Har Megiddo as a conductor of evil intent. He called on all good and faithful Christians to declare their faith in God's only child, Christ. He called on all world leaders to spare no expense in searching out and destroying the devil in his lair.

The Soviet Union congratulated the Holy See on its communique in general but took exception to the Pope's call that the said criminal be brought to the Vatican City to stand trial. They suggested a court be chosen from twelve nations in some world body, such as the United Nations.

It was reported from Switzerland that the Soviets were sending heavy shipments of arms to the Arab League nations.

India, China, Vietnam, North Korea, and Canada offered military equipment to the Arabs and said it was under study at the highest levels whether to offer direct military intervention to destroy once and for all the pariah nation in the Middle East—Israel!

The Arab Oil Cartel announced that there was a surplus of oil on the world market and that they had voted a reduction in the price of oil by a third of a cent per barrel.

The President of the United States announced shortly after receiving confirmation of the reduced oil prices that an arms embargo against Israel would go immediately into effect until the Israelis agreed to turn over the administration of the City of Jerusalem to the United Nations.

As the sun broke into pieces over the city of New York, Hamish and his little band of fugitives, running on impulse engines, were ushered quickly into the home of Sydney Schwartz.

At the same time, the Government of Israel warned the American Government of the dire consequences of the actions taken by the president.

The Prime Minister said that the City of Jerusalem wasn't negotiable. He repeated his warning to all aggressor nations that the people of Israel would protect their integrity by any means necessary. He underscored the words: "By any means!"

***

Happiness is? Happiness is? Not running for your life. From what or who or why he was running was a mystery to Harry. He asked no questions, and he received no explanations as to why he was being dragged from place to place.

It seemed to him that everything was clear to everyone but him. He sat on the bed, staring at the door, trying to decide whether it was locked from the inside or out.

He shuddered each time he heard his name mentioned in the other room. He was sure that whoever was out there had nothing nice to say about him—and wondered if they were listening to those who had brought him here -- "God!" He hid his head under the covers, feeling full of self-pity.

In the living room, the people crowded every square foot of the wall-to-wall carpeting. They came early in the day and stayed until late at night.

"Sidney," Hamish stridently took him to one side, "I thought you and I agreed that you weren't to tell anyone we were here; and then you said only a few; and now...!"

"It couldn't be helped," replied Syd, round and short, his head balding, long sideburns tapering down the side of his face. "What could I do? Put yourself in my place, Mr. Zahari. When my children came home from school, I had to tell them who was staying with us. And when they heard it was none other than Har Megiddo, the same fellow that's been on the news every night, I couldn't stop them in time from telling a few of their friends. It's late, and their parents couldn't let them out alone. You can understand that. And my wife...! When she got home from the beauty parlor and heard it was him—what could I do? Tear the phone out of the wall?"

"And who are they. And them? Those people over there?" Hamish's tongue shook with anger.

"That is my partner, Murray, and his wife and brother-in-law. I had to tell him! If I didn't and he found out later who was here, he would have sold out on me." He shook his head. "I'm sorry, I'm too old to have the patience to break in a new man. You know, the ladies apparel business isn't as easy as everyone seems to think! It takes a special talent for a man to sell undergarments to a woman. These are all my friends, the Rabbi and his wife and children, the president of my Synagogue, our family doctor, and his son, who, by the way, is a student at the Yeshiva."

"I give you my word of honor as a Jew and life-long and ardent supporter of Israel that none of my friends gathered here today in my house will breathe a word to anyone that you and he and the others are hiding here." He crossed his heart. "I swear it."

Exasperated, Hamish once more surveyed this man, his friends, and his family.

"I would be crazy," Syd's logic rambled on, "if I invited any whom I couldn't trust. I'm a lot of things, but never has it been said of Sydney Schwartz that he is stupid! If the police found you here.... I shudder at the thought. All of everything I have ever worked for would be down the drain."

"Sydney, you're a good, decent man," replied Hamish.

"But you just don't seem to get the point!"

"No, Hamish, it is you who don't understand! Now, don't get me wrong. I don't want you or anyone else to pay me back for the risks I and my family are taking on your and the others' behalf. But if you're inclined to do something nice in return, how about letting me and my friends get a peek at the great man? We're, I mean, they're... I've already seen him—and if you don't mind me saying so, he looks exactly as I thought he would. What do you say, Mr. Zahari? The others are anxious to see Har Megiddo, especially the children."

"I told you before," Hamish listened with a gaping mouth. "And you force me to explain it all to you once again. He's tired! He, I, and all of us are tired. Can't you ask your friends to leave so we can get some much-needed rest? Maybe tomorrow he'll be up to seeing visitors."

Hamish decided that long before tomorrow they'd be long gone from these people. He was going to gather Deborah and Al and get the hell out before his gracious host got them all arrested.

Not worrying about being rude, he turned away from Sydney and rushed his way across the room to where Harry was being kept. The door was locked. He knocked.

"Who's there?" He heard Deborah ask.

"It's me, Hamish. Let me in." He hurried in. "Al, I'm glad you're here."

"Why? What's up? Something wrong?"

"Yes... Everything! We're getting out of here."

"Now?"

"Now!"

"No..." whined Harry. "I'm tired. Where are you dragging me off to now? Can't it wait till morning?"

"No," snapped Hamish. "Can't you go along once without putting up an argument?"

The one window in the room was blocked by an air conditioner.

Hamish and Al, with a little help from Harry, very little help, lifted it out and set it quietly on the floor.

There was a knock at the door. "Hey in there..." It was Sydney. "What are you people doing in there? Open up! Let me in!" The door shook from his pounding. "It's my house!" What do you want?" Hamish urgently helped the others out the window. He followed at their heels, racing down the fire escape. They didn't slow down till they were blocks away.

"You get the car I told you to rent?" Hamish labored, out of breath.

"Sure did," Al replied. "Follow me. I parked it a few blocks away from here."

Squeezed by too many cups of coffee, Harry's bladder screamed with urgency.

"Hold on," sympathetically said Hamish. "We're almost there."

Harry grimaced, tucked his legs under himself, then straightened them straight out. He slipped down in his seat, then pushed himself erect. He squirmed from side to side, brushing into Al one too many times.

"Stop your squirming!" Al elbowed him in the ribs.

"Hurry," begged Harry for Deborah to speed the car up.

"I'm going the speed limit," she replied. "You don't want me to get stopped for speeding."

"Yes, no, I mean hurry! Please! I don't think I can hold it much longer!"

***

Irving and Donna Wishnatiski had a son, Sammy, who enveloped their home with pains and cries of agony. Once a beautiful child, now doomed by cancer slowly nibbling his life off the bone. Sammy was a gnarled and twisted little boy on the outside; on the inside, he roared with the courage of a lion.

As soon as he heard from his dad that Har Megiddo and his three companions were coming to stay a few days with them, Sammy argued and argued with his father till Irving gave in and

126

allowed him to stay up.

It had been months since Sammy had last been able to stand the pain of sitting up, but tonight, as Irving lifted the boy into his wheelchair, not a sound or whimper escaped between his lips. He was wheeled over to a living room window so he could watch for the Messiah. He had been there for hours already. Waiting…! Waiting…! Never taking his eyes off the street for more than a second or two.

"I'm not comfortable with this whole idea," said Donna worriedly. "He's built his hopes too high that this Megiddo will heal him, and you know as well as I, darling, that he might be a lot of things, but he's no Messiah."

"Let Sammy find hope where he may," replied a sober father. In the recesses of his mind, he never dared tell his wife that he prayed for his son's merciful death. "What harm can it do?"

Donna and Irving were about to tear at each other's hearts when a happy cry gave them pause.

"He's coming!" Sammy shook his wheelchair. "He's coming! He's coming!" He shouted with joy.

"The Lord's coming!"

"He is…?" they exclaimed, coming to stand by their son. "Where?"

"The Lord," answered the youth, pointing out in the street. "The Messiah! There he is!"

They looked. The sun was coming down behind a layer of dark clouds; dew drops were settling on petals of flowers. A man could be seen coming up onto the porch. He was dressed in dark colors. He was holding his coat over his face. A beetle tripped over a twig and tumbled out of his way.

"My heart is going to burst, Mother," Sammy exclaimed, grinning from ear to ear. "I believe it's him."

"Which one?"

"Shh..., don't talk… And who are all those others with him, father?"

"Friends of Har Megiddo's," replied Irving. He watched his son closely. "Sammy, I don't want you getting your hopes too high. We don't know for sure that he is the one." Irving was sure he wasn't but didn't say anything.

"He is! He is, I know it, Father! I do!"

The doorbell chimed. Irving went to let their guests in. He hesitated with his hand on the doorknob. "Now take it easy," he said to Sammy. "You've had a full day, and I don't want you to over-excite yourself."

"I promise." Sammy was wheeled by his mother to face the door.

Irving opened the door. "Mr. Wishnatski?"

"Yes."

"I'm Hamish Zahari. I called earlier. I believe you were expecting us."

"Yes, yes," he gaped at Harry, then at Al, wondering which one of them he was.

"May we come in?"

"Yes, of course, pardon me." He stepped aside and allowed them by. "You have to pardon my manners. It's been a long day."

"For all of us," replied Hamish. "I know what you mean. It is good of you to put us up." Hamish slipped off his coat. "Not many would take the risks. You and your family are brave people."

"Not so brave," Irving replied. "Ordinary people we are. Here," he reached out. "Let me have your coats."

Harry wasn't interested in taking his coat off. All he wanted to know was: where was the bathroom? All any of the others could see of him were his eyes and forehead, his nose sticking out between the buttons of his coat.

"Please, sir," said Harry. "May I use your bathroom?" He crossed his legs in front of himself, squeezing his thighs together.

"Yes, of course. You're a guest; no need to ask

128

permission. My home is yours." He pointed Harry down the hallway. "It's the third door to your left."

With nothing further to say, Harry quickly made his way to the bathroom.

Al nodded at Hamish and followed after. He opened the bathroom door a crack and waited outside.

That made Irving uneasy, but he said nothing.

"I take it," said Hamish, "that this is your wife."

"And my son," said Irving. "And who, might I ask, is this charming woman?"

"I'm Deborah," she replied for herself.

"I'm Donna. Glad to meet you," she smiled.

Sammy was having problems sitting up in his chair. He tried hiding the pain he felt, but he couldn't fool his mother.

"Sammy, I think you've been up long enough for one day."

"Oh Mother," he pleaded. "Please! Please! Let me wait to see Har Megiddo once more." He looked to his father.

"I believe your mother's right," he said. "It's time for you to rest now."

"Oh, father!"

"No more argument," tenderly, Irving looked on his son. What a brave little boy, trying his best to hide the pain he felt from his folks.

***

"Go to bed, and if Mr. Megiddo's not too tired, I'll bring him in to say goodnight—and if not, tomorrow will come soon enough."

Deborah watched Irving closely and saw clearly the pain between the lines in his face as Donna wheeled Sammy off to bed.

"My son's terminal," Irving turned back to his guests. "The doctors gave him a few months, give or take a month. He lives by the grace of God, or in grace, as you will. Sammy has bone cancer, very painful. My son, Mr. Zahari, has the only courage left in this house."

"We come then," replied Hamish, "at a bad time."

"No... No...! To tell you and the others have come at a good time. Can I be completely honest with you?"

"Please be."

"My son knows he's dying." Irving wiped his sweaty palms on his pants. Donna came back, and he waited for her to tell him about Sammy.

"I gave him his medicine." Tiredly, she slouched. "He'll be asleep shortly."

"I was telling our guests about Sammy, darling."

"Go on." She understood that it was important to let their guests in on what they had walked into. 'If I were in their shoes,' she thought to herself, 'I'd get out of here as quick as I could.'

"My wife and I are reconciled to the fact that anytime he might pass away. But Sammy, he has never lost hope—and when he heard about Har Megiddo and that he was coming here, you might well imagine his reaction."

"You have to say no more, Mr. Wishnatski. I get the picture. Your son believes that Harry is the Messiah and he can do for him what everyone else says is impossible," Hamish whistled through his teeth. "I'm afraid to tell you folks that our Harry is no Messiah. He can work about as many miracles as you or I or any of us."

"I never thought any different," replied Irving. "I was hoping to give my son a few days of happiness, and if your friend would go along...? Play the role of our Saviour? I and my wife would deeply appreciate it to the end of our days."

"I can't speak for him," said Hamish. "You'll have to ask Harry yourself. But I have to tell you..."

"Here comes Al with Harry now," interrupted Deborah.

Donna suggested that everyone retire into the living room and make themselves comfortable while she fixed up a bite to eat. "You all look half-starved."

"We are," Deborah took to Donna right off. "Famished! I'll help if you don't mind."

Irving watched Harry closely. He wanted to see what kind of man he had to appeal to. Harry showed his fatigue; his posture was sloppy. Great strain was pulling one eye lower than the other, or was it the long, nasty scratch under his left eye causing him to blink rapidly? But that was nothing compared to the irritating noise made by Harry grinding his teeth together.

Irving debated. He had his doubts whether, even if Harry went along with his plan, he might not do his son more harm than good.

Al was saying, "Jews have had it here in America. They're kidding themselves if they believe it will ever be the way it was again. I'm telling you, the writing's clearly on the wall."

"If it is and you're right," replied Hamish, "it's sad not just for American Jews and Israelis, but for all freedom-loving people everywhere."

Irving wanted to think of something else to give himself a rest from worrying about Sammy. He joined in on the conversation. "I'm an American—been one all my life. Second generation and all that. And I must say that, in my opinion, there are no more generous and noble people in all the world. America has been and still is the best friend Jews have ever had."

"I see...," sarcastically replied Al. "You make a distinction between American Jews and Israeli Jews, the latter being expendable to preserve the former."

"I said no such thing," defensively replied Irving. "You've twisted what I've said all out of proportion. What do you think?" He asked Harry. "Do you believe that the American people are turning against Jewish people?"

Harry wasn't listening. He was off in a world of his own, dreaming of a time and a place where all words have been said, all lovers loved, all dreams have been dreamt, all science discovered, and everything that was supposed to have happened has happened, when God is dead and man becomes God.

"Why ask him?" said Al with a madness that surprised everyone. "He's no Jew! He doesn't care what becomes of us. It's no concern of his. He's too stupid to even know what's going on around him, that he's being used by others to try once again and destroy us as a people!"

"Me...?" Harry pointed an accusing finger at himself.

"Yes," snapped Al. "You, you're a red flag waving at the bulls, and the bulls can't understand that the flag isn't what threatens them. It's the sliver of steel hiding behind it, poised for the kill!"

"Me...?" Harry honestly didn't have the faintest idea what Al was yelling about. He pressed his finger into his chest till it hurt. "Why me? What have I done? I haven't done nothing."

"Hamish put his finger on it before," said Al, a little calmer but no less fervent.

"I did...?"

"You did. Remember when you said that it didn't make any difference whether Harry was or wasn't the Messiah? It only mattered what people believed?"

"Yes... but...?"

"But nothing! The truth is the truth, whether you want to believe it or not! The powerful are whipping up their people's passions in almost every country against Jews. Harry's their red flag. It's been waived before. He's a symbol, standing for all of us." Al's voice cracked with anger. "Every time they kill a Jew, they kill Harry! I believe that they have no intention of finding him until we've all been exterminated!"

Donna came into the room, carrying the food. She laughed. "You men can't leave the room for one minute before you're arguing about who knows what. You'd think you've known each other all your lives. The way you're at each other's throats!"

"Nobody argues like a Jew." Deborah followed, balancing gingerly a tray full of steaming hot coffee. "I knew a Jewish gentleman once who would walk ten miles to find another Jew so he could get into an argument."

"And Jewish women are different from their men?" laughed Irving.

"Oh yes." Deborah handed him a sandwich. "The difference is that it wouldn't make a hoot of difference to us, Jew, Christian, or atheist; we'd argue with all without prejudice."

Everyone laughed heartily but Harry. "Aren't you hungry?" Donna asked, sad that he seemed to be such an unhappy man.

"No ma'am," he muttered. "I'm not feeling too good."

"Not again," exasperated said Al. "You're the most complaining person I have ever had the misfortune of meeting."

"I see nothing wrong with asking for a little sympathy," indignantly said Donna. "Everyone's entitled to a little stroking once in a while."

"You don't understand, Mrs. Wishnatski," replied Al. "We don't haven't the time or the energy to be wasted coddling him. The hell with him! What we have to do is to get as many Jews out of the country before it's too late. Fortify Israel! Mobilize the people! Store up food and arms. Do what we must, no matter what it is! We must survive!"

"I still don't understand," mumbled Harry, sorry he had spoken before the words were hardly off his tongue. "What do I have to do with all that?"

"What do you have to do with all that?" Amazed, Irving stared incredulously at Hamish. "He's kidding? Isn't he?"

"No, I don't believe he is."

"My God! Don't you know?" exclaimed Irving.

"No!" Harry trembled, his nose dripping freely down his chin.

He made no attempt to wipe himself.

Donna went over and sat next to Harry. She took his hand in hers. "Poor baby! Now you men stop this! You're being vicious!"

"He has to find out sooner or later," said Hamish, calmly. "No sense in letting him go on living in ignorance."

"What...," cried Harry. "What is happening?"

"You're being accused of every rape, murder, robbery, and every lousy, stinking calamity in the world," hollered Al. His voice fell and rose from peaks to valleys with wild abandonment. "The fever runs wild once again in the small minds of men. You're in a hundred different places all at the same time. You're everything to everyone. You're tall and short depending on where you live. Your eyes are blue in Sweden and green in Greece. You have a beard in the Soviet Union. You're clean-shaven in West Germany. Your hair is brown in Pakistan, dark and wavy in Italy; in Zaire, it's short and curly."

"When we stopped for coffee earlier today," added Deborah, "I overheard one of the waitresses telling a customer that in Albania, you are accused of being a provocateur, that you gunned down a hundred women and children in cold blood."

"I did no such thing," Harry sat up straight. "that's crazy, and you know it. I have never been out of the city till I met you people."

"I believe you," said Donna. "You know why? Because at the same time you were being accused in Albania, you were positively identified in Australia as a petty thief, robbing two nuns of their crucifixes!"

"I don't believe you." Harry misunderstood and pushed Donna away.

"I don't believe any of you! Why?"

"You don't! You don't!" Irving worked himself into a frenzy. He reached under the sofa and pulled out the evening newspaper and slammed it down in Harry's lap. "You can read, can't you!"

Harry nodded and sank back into the sofa.

"The whole damn front page is about you. United Press International reports from Champaign, Illinois: 'The Enema Bandit Strikes Again! Late last night, a masked bandit robbed and terrified a University of Illinois coed in her apartment. Before he left, the bandit tied his victim up, stripped her naked, and gave her an enema. The police Chief said that a positive identification has been made of the pervert, and it matched the F.B.I's composite photo of one Harry Megiddo. Six feet six inches tall, two hundred and twenty-five pounds, long straight black hair that falls down to the shoulders. He was last seen wearing sandals, no socks, torn faded blue jeans, and a work shirt."'

Harry cried out. "You all feel better now that you've yelled at me? I never did no harm to anyone in my life. Anyways, I don't fit the Enema Man's description."

"You're impossibly thick," replied a more composed Al. "He refuses to face the truth. There are at least a dozen rewards out on your head. The world's a mess, and once again they turn on Jews!"

Irving calmed down too. "Take small comfort, Harry. It isn't only you that they hunt. Innocents everywhere are falling in your wake."

"And from Israel?" Deborah wanted to know. "What news do you have?"

"I know only what I read in the papers," Irving replied. "Most foreigners have left or are leaving the country. Most governments have pulled out their embassies, all except the Netherlands and the United States."

"That's all? Nothing more? What do the people think of our friend, Harry?"

"Yes. I have read that many Israelis have had a change of heart about Har Megiddo. They demand that the government bring our friend here home safe and sound."

Harry sighed quietly.

"Harry has become something of a national pride," said Irving. "I can't believe that most folks actually believe Harry's the Messiah, but they do see him, like you said, as a red flag. They hear of his deeds, risking his life for others, coming to the rescue of persecuted Jews all over the world, at great risk to his own life. Alas, Harry has become sort of a folk hero to most Israelis."

"Me... I'm no Messiah..."

Hamish laughed, breaking the last of the tension in the room. "That, Harry," he chuckled, "we all agree on."

Irving wiped his mouth. "I'm sorry, Harry, I had no right to yell at you. I don't know what came over me."

"Me too," said Donna. Harry said nothing when she squeezed his hand.

"Gee," she suggested, "I think we've all had a long day. Why don't we call it a night? I've fixed up a place for all of you."

— CHAPTER FOURTEEN —

Happens to be the day before tomorrow. It's next door to September. The Holy Land is experiencing the worst heat wave in recorded history. No end is in sight, and the temperatures are expected to climb further tomorrow. How much? The experts refuse to predict. All anyone can do is wait and keep their minds on something other than the heat. Most people turn their attention to Har Megiddo.

And Yeshaayia Gurevich, taunted and jeered for the best part of his life, ignored for the worst, was now followed by a great multitude of admirers wherever the spirit moved him.

His smile had become famous throughout the land. He grinned from ear to ear as a slight wind tickled his fancy.

The multitude was silenced.

"The prophesied day draws near. Open your ears. Open your hearts, brothers and sisters. The God of Israel sends me unto you with glad tidings. The Kingdom of Heaven is coming!"

A great roar of approval came from the mouths of the people.

"I rejoice! I rejoice!" shouted Yeshaayia with happiness. "I rejoice because only last night, the Lord opened the door of my temple and entered my mind, promising that I would live to see his spirit, Har Megiddo, work his miracle in the desert."

"We believe! We believe you, Yeshaayia," the gathered crowd changed. "Glory to you! Glory to Har Megiddo! Deliverer of Israel! Destroy our enemies, but quickly, while we are still alive!"

"Make way for Nadab! Make way for Nadab, the butcher!" Nadab hollering, came running through the crowd.

"The Rabbi is dead!" He shouted his announcement. "Rabbi Tzadikovich is dead!" The people cleared a path for him to the Prophet.

"Oh, my God!" He grasped the butcher around the legs.

137

"Is it true, Nadab?" he cried. "Tell me it isn't?"

"It is true, most honored one."

"Really, you swear to God?"

"I swear it," he replied. "The Rabbi, half his heart turned to fat, couldn't support his great bulk any longer. He dropped dead in his cell a few hours ago."

The people shouted, "Hurray! Hurray!" They jumped up and down, swung their loved ones around, kissed, and wept with strangers.

"The Rabbi is dead! Hurray, hurray!"

Yeshaayia raised himself erect with much difficulty. "Oh no, good friends!" He shouted for them to be silent. "No... No rejoicing. The death of our Rabbi Tzadikovich is a cause of great sorrow. The Rabbi alone kept the flame alive while I, for so many years, lost my way. Noo...! I beseech you, mourn Rabbi Tzadikovich with all the honors and glory you would bestow on any of our great teachers. Mourn him for six days and nights, and on the seventh day, the new day of rest for the Lord, I see the Messiah sitting on the throne of David. I see a new world beginning in all its innocence, running over with God's stream of life. I see a people in every nook and cranny of the world losing their identities and becoming one with Har Megiddo. I see a world of justice, I see with mine eyes," Yeshaayia's voice floated over the assembled. "I see Har Megiddo, tall and strong, good and kind, wise and patient, ruling over all God's children."

***

A cloud of smoke was ignored, moving west from the east coast of America. Spotted with the naked eye, plotted on every radar screen, more dangerous than a speeding bullet, quicker than a train, carried gently in the arms of the wind, touching every square inch of the firmament.

If any citizen of the planet earth had bothered to squat down and press an ear to the ground, listen carefully... The old world was huffing and puffing, laboring to breathe. The picture was darkening. The wind blew a stink. The very air trembled with expectation for the children. The soil was spoiled when the children grew up. The old planet was wheezing, about to have enough.

Early in the morning, the haze was thicker than usual. Harry, sleeping on the screened-in porch, was awakened by a dewdrop falling on his nose. It tickled. He listened closely. There were no sounds of anyone else moving about the house yet. He opened one eye and through the slit saw Hamish fast asleep. He had slept in his clothes and was up in a shot, ready to go. He opened and closed the screen door quietly and crept on his tiptoes, holding his breath, along the side of the house. He ducked under a window, thinking he had it made, when suddenly, he heard someone calling, "Are you the Messiah?" He froze.

"I can't get out of bed on my own, but if you want to, you can climb through the window."

"Who… Who's that?" Harry, frightened, stuttered.

"It's me, Sammy."

"Who?"

"Sammy. Don't you remember me?"

Harry peered cautiously through the open window. There, lying in a hospital bed, was that same little boy he saw in the wheelchair last night.

"Sure, I remember you," he said so as not to hurt Sammy's feelings.

"How could I forget a head of curly hair like yours?"

Sam winced.

"Is something the matter?" Harry leaned through the window. "You in pain?" He climbed in the room.

"Noo…" replied Sammy, forcing a smile. "I was afraid you were leaving without stopping to see me."

"You would have cared?"

"I would have cared very much," Sammy replied. "Ever since father told me you were coming, I haven't been able to think of anything else."

"I wasn't going anywhere in particular," Harry stretched the truth. "I was just taking a walk, stretching my legs. Nobody else is up, and I was bored."

"Do you know of any games we could play?" said Sammy, pulling himself up with obvious effort.

"I play a game with myself sometimes when I'm real lonely." Harry grabbed a pillow and slid it behind Sammy's back. "Here, take my hand. Can you guess what I'm thinking?"

"Oh yes! Let me try!" Sammy closed his eyes. "Hey! It's all dark in here," he giggled.

"Why, sure it is. You're silly," said Harry. "Squeeze your eyes tighter and behold, above your head, the stars glitter and glow, lighting you a path to follow."

"I see," exclaimed Sammy. "There goes the dark; here comes a light. God almighty, it's beautiful! What is it?"

"Your mind," replied Harry. "Hello... Say hello, Sammy."

"Hello..."

"Now you can travel anywhere your heart desires. All you have to do is want to go, Sammy. When I was your age, I used to travel to far and distant places. I fought Apaches side by side with Buffalo Bill. One time, I remember, I was the King of Siam; another time I was the proud owner of a chocolate factory, and all the other boys and girls came to play with me. Oh... Sammy, some of the best times I ever had. I never had to leave my room."

"I can do it, I can, I know it!" Sammy squeezed his eyes tighter. "My bed is disappearing," he said, full of wonder. "I'm standing on nothing, with no help from anybody. My body feels wonderful. See here, I can stick my hand through my chest, and even that doesn't hurt!"

"You've done it," exclaimed Harry loudly. "My God, you've done it, you have! Now...! Who would dare say that my friend Sammy can't get around on his own?"

The door opened unexpectedly, and in came Sammy's

mother. "Sammy!" said Donna angrily.

"What are you doing?" She hurried over to him. "Don't you know better than to excite yourself like this?"

"Oh mommy," beamed Sammy. "You don't understand." He tried explaining, but she just wouldn't listen.

"And you," she snapped at Harry. "You for sure should have more sense!"

"Oh mommy," said Sammy, throwing his arms around her neck, planting kisses over her face. "Don't yell at him! He's the Messiah, don't you know?"

***

It was near midday. Donna and Irving, deathly flushed, had been arguing all day.

"You weren't there. You didn't hear his tone of voice or see his face. You know what he said to me? He said that if I didn't believe Harry was the Messiah, I was stupid!"

"He didn't mean it."

"Oh yes he did! He said that I wasn't going in the right direction to see Harry clearly. Sammy said that if I was kind and generous, if I did noble deeds, then I would see him for what he is. He said that because I have been unkind to Harry, because I'm afraid of everything, the Messiah turns his true face away from me."

Donna buried her face in her hands and sobbed. "What have I done to our son to cause him to side with a stranger over his mother?"

"Donna! You're going to have to pull yourself together. What am I going to do with you? I think you think too much about yourself." He caught his thought falling off his tongue. He sounded harsher than he had intended.

"And...?" Donna knew the truth but wanted him to say it. "And what else...?" she insisted.

"It's been many a morning since last our son has apparently felt as good. Could it be—I'm not saying it is—that you feel bitter towards Harry because he's able to accomplish

141

what we seem unable to do anymore? Take Sammy's mind off his hurts and pains; help him forget for a while his miseries?"

"What happens if our son finds out the truth? That Harry isn't a Messiah any more than I am? Even his companions admit to that!"

"I believe," replied Irving, "that Sammy knows the truth. He's taken the bitter and set it aside. He chooses to believe, to pretend, living in a fantasy where he's a normal boy with normal aches and pains. Harry comforts him, exhorts him to fantasize, and makes it all the more real for him. And I might add that we were going to ask Harry ourselves to go along with Sammy, if you remember. The only crime Harry's committed is that he isn't the Messiah, and we certainly can't blame him for that!"

Donna was down so low that up was out of sight. "I don't know what to think anymore! All I want is what's best for Sammy."

"I know, I know!" He took her in his arms. "I know, dearest. I never doubted that for a second."

"Wouldn't it be something," wistfully said Donna, "if he turned out to be the Messiah?"

"I'm afraid we're not children," he replied. "But if Harry makes our Sammy happy, then to me he is the Messiah."

***

The humidity was oppressive. Dark and dingy day all around. Once more today, Harry stayed by Sammy's side, never leaving the bedroom except for an occasional trip to the bathroom. Late in the afternoon, Irving and Donna went hand in hand into see their son. Nothing has been seen of them since.

Al paced back and forth, his hands twisting together behind his back. "I don't like it! Not one bit! This place gives me the jitters!"

"Easy does it." Hamish looked up from his newspaper. "This is as good a place as we're going to find till this fuss about Harry dies down."

"I'm beginning to get worried myself," said Deborah.

"It's been a good while since last we had contact with our people."

"I'm sure," Hamish replied, "that they haven't forgotten us. They're waiting, I bet, for the right moment."

"You think so?"

"I really do! Listen to this," he opened the newspaper. "They're accusing the followers of Har Megiddo, in collusion with the government, of desecrating shrines holy to both Christians and Moslems. The Pope has said that he would use all the powers at his command to force the Jews to surrender the Holy City of Jerusalem into the hands of a Christian International body."

"Never...!" Furiously, Al said to Hamish. "Never! I'd sooner see Jerusalem utterly destroyed!"

"Keep your voice down!" Hamish rolled his eyes till they stopped at the top of his head. "You don't want to give the man upstairs any ideas."

"I would if I could, and I'd tell him to kill our enemies. I'd scream at him, haven't we had enough? Haven't we paid for whatever we did in the first place? Can't we ever live in peace and tranquility?"

"I'm afraid that if Jews are going to find peace on this earth, in this lifetime," said Deborah, "we're going to have to fight for it!"

"I don't know..." Hamish fastened his eyes on his daughter. "Sometimes, I think, fighting for peace is like making love for virginity. You make love; you have babies sooner or later. You fight; sooner or later, someone gets killed, a lot of young men and women get killed, all losers."

"You want to know what else is making me nervous?" Al stared down the hallway in the direction of Sammy's room. "Them! What in the heck they doing in there?"

Hamish shrugged, "I don't know. They have been in there for an awfully long time. Let's go see."

The house was quiet. It was spooky. The only sounds to

be heard were the squeaking of their footsteps as they made their way to Sammy's room.

Hamish hesitated before opening the door. He heard talking from within. He listened for a few seconds, then pushed the door open. From the hallway, they peered in.

There in bed was Sammy, the covers pulled up over his shoulders, his head raised by pillows. He was talking in whispers. All the happiness, along with the sorrows he had lived through, showed clearly on his face.

"I'm a bird!" Sammy flapped his arms.

"An eagle," replied his father, "soaring through the sky on a clear blue day, as free as the wind that blows up above."

"Yo ho! Yo ho!" gleamed Sammy. "I can feel the wind in my face."

"It's cool and sweet-smelling," added his mother. "Do you see it yet, Sammy? It's the ocean."

"Oh yes, I do, I do!" He sat up, the covers falling down off his shoulders, showing a scar running down from his neck to his waist.

"I'm going to swoop down and have a look around. I want to say hello to my friends, the fish."

"Hello, there," Sammy hollered. "Hello, there. How are you on this fine day?" He swooped lower and landed on the back of a porpoise.

"And how are you this fine day?" the porpoise replied.

"I'm fine," Sammy laughed with joy. "I feel better today than I ever remember feeling."

"Hold on to me tightly," said the porpoise. "I want to show you something."

"What is it?"

"You'll see!" The porpoise leaped in the air. Sammy hung on for all he was worth, whooping and hollering, having a wondrous time. And all around, hundreds of other fish jumping in the air, seeing which one could jump the highest, go the fastest, sing the loudest, and dive the deepest. Then suddenly!

The porpoise slammed on the brakes, skidding its fins on the surface of the ocean. Sammy, the eagle, wings spread, fluttered up, up, up in the air.

"This is where the world ends," announced the porpoise. "Over there," he pointed a fin. "Beyond the horizon, the ocean falls off the earth. There you will find what you've been searching for. Farewell, Sammy! Fare-thee-well...!" The porpoise dove and soon disappeared.

Sammy, floating on an air current, taking him towards life's edge, looked back at his parents.

"Wait...! Wait...!" Donna cried. "Wait a while longer. We have so much to do, so much to see. Stay a little while longer. Don't leave me!" She beseeched.

"You're an eagle," his father hoarsely said. "You have been a good son. Fly on! Be proud and remember your father and mother have always and will always love you."

"Sound the trumpets," Harry, who had remained to one side for most of the day, yelled. "Sound the trumpets. Death is not a door that closes! It is a door that opens. He must enter. Sound the trumpets to let them know that Sammy is coming!"

Donna wailed loud enough to waken even the cantankerous God of the Jews. The day ended, squeezed by gloom. Harry felt jealous of where Sammy was at and would not go back in the room. He twiddled his fingers in the corner of the living room, making a conscious effort to be small, tiny, insignificant, or non-existent in the eyes of the others. Irving and Donna sat by their son. Donna was quietly sobbing into her handkerchief, feeling more sorry for herself than her son. Across from her, Irving felt guilty. His wish had been granted. Sammy was finally resting in peace.

Moonbeams cracked the heavens. "Where do we go from here?" Deborah in a low voice said to Al. "We can't stay here for much longer with the boy dead. The doctor has to be called, the police. This house is going to be crawling with strangers."

"Mr. Wishnatski has agreed not to call anyone in until we're safely away," replied Al. "He says it is the least he can do for Harry after all he has done for Sammy. I don't get it, but who wants to argue with him at a time like this?"

"Let them believe whatever they want," replied Deborah. "They're nice people, and if it helps them to believe in Harry, who are we to tell them they're crazy and add to their grief? I think…" She stopped in mid-thought upon seeing her father coming back in the room.

"Okay," he rubbed his hands vigorously together. "It's all set. I made contact with our people, and they're sending someone to get us now. Get your things together. They said they would be here in less than an hour."

"Thank God," Deborah rose up.

"Debby," said Hamish. "Hold it for a second." He had a scowl across his face. "Sit down. I want you to listen to me carefully. I'm going to tell you something you're not going to like, and I don't want any arguments from you."

"I can tell I'm not going to like it, but I'll take my medicine standing if you don't mind."

He shook his head. "You're not coming along. I've talked with Irving and Donna, and they have agreed to put you up till it's safe for you to leave the country."

"Noo…!" Deborah came nose to nose with her father. "Noo…!" She stamped her foot. "I won't be left behind."

"My mind is made up." Hamish didn't want to take any more chances. "Too many crazy things have happened since we ran into Harry. I'm adamant! I'm not going to take any more chances with your life, and that's final!"

Deborah argued and argued but to no avail. "You can't believe that he's the Messiah?" She glared at Harry.

"She's even blaming her having to stay on me," thought Harry. "If given the chance, I'd trade places with her in a second."

"No, I don't! It wouldn't make any difference if I did," replied Hamish. "Half the world is searching for him. I won't have you getting caught in the crossfire. That's all!"

"Please," she begged. "I don't want to leave you!"

"Can't be helped. In a few days, a couple of weeks, we'll all be laughing at this safely in Israel."

"No… Please…!" She looked to Al.

"I kinda agree with Hamish. If you're asking my opinion, I think maybe he's right. Look at it this way. The police are searching for three men and a woman. I believe it's a good idea if we split up. If my brother Ashel were still alive, I'm sure he would have suggested it long before now."

"But what about all the people—the doctor, the police, coming to the house?"

"You're the Wishnatski's niece," Hamish replied. "Come to help the family out in their time of grief. No one will question that."

A few minutes later, earlier than he had been expected, there was a heavy, urgent knock at the door.

"Who's there?" Hamish went over.

"It's a friend," came a reply. "You have been expecting me. I'm a friend of Zion."

Hamish opened the door, and the stranger pushed by nervously. "Something the matter?" Hamish closed and fastened the latch behind him.

"I wouldn't be surprised," he replied. "The way events have been going for Jews lately, nothing would surprise me."

"Hi," Irving held out his hand in greeting. "My name's Irving Wishnatiski, and this is my wife, Donna."

"Names are not important!" He brushed Irv's hand aside. "In my business, you can never be too careful."

Irving frowned.

"Heard about your son. My sincerest condolences."

"Thanks."

"No need to thank me," he replied. "In these times, all us Jews have to stick together. Here!" He turned to Hamish and handed him a large manila envelope.

"What's this?"

"It's everything you'll need but luck to get out of the country. Passports, papers, money. You all better study them thoroughly so you'll know your new identities."

"When do we go?" asked Al.

"Not for a few more days," he replied. "We're waiting to see if the heat dies down."

"Not for a few more days!" Al couldn't believe his ears. "I thought Hamish explained to you that it is impossible for us to hide here any longer."

"He has, he has! Don't get your dander up. It's all been arranged. From here, I'll take you to a place of safety. Don't worry. You'll be in the good hands of the Jewish Defense League."

"What...?" stammered Hamish. He didn't like the sound of that one bit.

"Now, you hold on, buster! I'm one of those people you're turning your nose up at! You couldn't be in safer or more trustworthy hands. You have no idea how famous you've become. Strangers stop strangers on the streets to see if they can spot Har Megiddo and collect the numerous bounties out on his head. Nobody wants to touch you people with a ten-foot pole. We're all you have, and you're damn lucky at that!"

"Easy does it," advised Al to Hamish. "We have many other choices."

"I guess not." Hamish stole a glance over at Harry, who was crouching in the corner.

"I take it," the stranger followed Hamish's eyes, "that that's him, Har Megiddo." He walked slowly over. "You don't look much like I pictured you would." He circled around.

Harry shrugged, wishing to himself that he could disappear. He was tired, so very tired. He resolved to be a nothing from here on out. It wouldn't be difficult, he thought. 'I've been a nothing all my life.'

He said in a whisper, "I'll go along with whatever

Hamish decides to do."

Hamish decided to go along. He had very little choice, as had been so aptly pointed out to him by Al. His one consolation was that his daughter was staying behind, and she would be as safe as any Jew could expect to be these hard days.

"Hamish," Irving stopped him at the door. "Don't worry, I'll take good care of Deborah. We'll treat her as if she were our own daughter. Donna and I have decided that as soon as we've buried our son, we'll take Deborah to Israel ourselves."

"Takes a load off my mind." Hamish shook Irv's hand warmly. He kissed Donna on the cheek tenderly. Giving his daughter one long last look, he forced himself to turn away, beating down a horrible thought that he would never see Deborah again.

Harry followed closely at Hamish's heels out of the house, Al pressing his hand on his back. Harry brushed aside Irving's gratitude without replying.

"Thank you." Harry heard Donna call his name. "Thank you, Har Megiddo, and Godspeed."

Out onto the street they came. They were led to a car parked right outside. Got in and pulled away. They had not driven a hundred feet when the shrill sounds of sirens blared in their ears. There, through the rearview window, they saw clearly a half dozen or so police cars pulling up in front of the Wishnatski's house.

"You must have been followed," hollered Al.

The only reply he got was the car speeding up.

"Deborah..." yelled Hamish, opening the door. He got one foot out before Al grabbed hold of his arm and dragged him back in.

"There's nothing you can do," he screamed in Hamish's face. "Nothing!" He reached over Hamish and slammed the car door shut.

"God damn you...!" Al grabbed hold of Harry and shook him furiously. "God damn you...!"   What kind of man are you?!"

— CHAPTER FIFTEEN —

A way in the distance, shofars trumpeted the sorrow of the Hebrews. The hordes once again were banging at their door. Har Megiddo was their only salvation. The corpse of Rabbi Tzadikovich had been laid to rest in a plain pine coffin, drawn through the streets of Jerusalem in a wooden cart, pulled by a broken-down ass. The Prophet Yeshaayia led the ass by the nose through the winding tangle of narrow cobblestone streets and dark arcades, passing jumbles of stone houses which had been the Rabbi's battleground for most of his life.

Hundreds of people fell in behind the procession, which wound for dozens of blocks. Yeshaayia led the funeral march to a stone courtyard. In the Center stood the Mosque of Omar, crowned by a golden dome, decorated in Persian tiles that sparkled green, blue and gold.

Today was Friday, and hundreds of tense and angry Arab Moslems flocked to pray near and in the Mosque. They stared angrily at the strange funeral procession that was desecrating their holy ground. To the east of the Great Mosque, Solomon had built his temple, and part of the Eastern wall of the courtyard still stands. Hundreds of Jews were already gathered; hundreds more had followed in behind Yeshaayia. Standing between the Jews and the Arabs, a detail of Israeli soldiers stood guard. The Jews felt good about the army being there; the Arabs were antagonized further. They pushed in on the center of the funeral procession, heaping abuse on Yeshaayia.

The Jews shouted back, "Make way for the Prophet. Out of the way," they hollered, "you dirty Arabs!"

The way was blocked. Yeshaayia and the dead Rabbi were surrounded by infuriated people. The soldiers were forced back against the cart. They started swinging their weapons in a wide arc.

The wagon tumbled over, and the casket slid out on the ground. Somebody screamed that the Arabs were trying to steal the Rabbi's body. Shots were fired! People were hollering! Pandemonium... Jews and Arabs tripped over each other in their frantic haste to get out of the line of fire. Reinforcements came, and soon the sounds of battle were far off in the distance, playing the chorus to the lead of the bloody wounded left lying in the courtyard.

Yeshaayia was unharmed, except for a long scratch down his cheek, which opened and bled each and every time he smiled. He sat spread-legged on top of the casket. To him, what he saw was further proof that the Messiah was coming. 'The closer he comes, the more desperate the devil becomes. Let the devil have his last stand,' he thought. 'It will get a lot worse before it gets any better.'

A couple of soldiers righted the cart. Yeshaayia stood out of the way while they lifted the casket back into the wagon.

"Gently," Yeshaayia smiled, wiping the blood from his cheek. "Gently..." The blood dripped through his fingers. "Gently..." His hand shook, splattering blood over the soldiers and cart.

A few minutes later, Yeshaayia led the ass by the nose out of the courtyard, surrounded by a detail of soldiers with orders to keep the procession moving.

The cemetery was ringed by more soldiers, in some places two or three thick, keeping the overflow of curious, devout, and tourists back.

Yeshaayia stood over the open grave and watched sadly as the grave diggers lowered the Rabbi into his resting place. "Here lies the Rabbi," he said. "He has given his life in the service of the Lord. Who here today could have asked any more of him?" Not a word or a sound came forth.

"The Rabbi is in grace," shouted Yeshaayia, his voice cracking with emotion. "Har Megiddo is his legacy!" He cried as the first shovel of dirt was thrown into the grave by one of the faithful Guardians of Jerusalem. "His term on earth is over. The standard bearer comes. Rally Judeans under the banner of David, carried by the Messiah. He died" - He held his trembling, blood-caked hand in the air—"so "Har Megiddo may live for all of us."

Where once Yeshaayia's message fell on deaf ears, today it was gobbled up by thousands. A hoopoe bird landed on his shoulder. A great wind arose from nowhere, slapping the mourners and soldiers to the ground. But he was standing, and not a strand of hair was blown out of place.

They hollered for help.

"Prophet, do you not care if the wind breaks our bones?"

Later, the story ran wild through the city that the Prophet Yeshaayia scolded the wind.

"Peace! Be still!" And the wind died away, and there came a great calm.

"Who then is this?" - No one could talk of anything else—"That commands even the wind?"

***

Ertz Israel was steaming at her seams, pointed sharp needles stuck in her from within as well as without. For whom had her armies been put on a high state of alert; for whom was a curfew imposed on Arab towns and villages; for whom were the nations of the world pointing an accusing finger at the people of Israel, denouncing them as warmongering and racist—for whom?

For Harry Megiddo, who at this very moment was throwing thunderbolts at processions of men and women who filed by for miles through his head.

He sat slouched on a stool in the middle of a sterile room. God only knew where. A light glared in his eyes. He had a miserable headache. He was surrounded by goons threatening his life unless he answered all their questions.

How many times had he begged them for water? He lost count. How many times did he have to tell them he wasn't a C.I.A. agent, Soviet spy, or bought by the Arab sheikhs to wreak havoc on Jews? How many times had they slapped him in the face? How many times had they stomped on his toes?

"How many times, for God sake, do I gotta tell you? I

didn't do any of those things!" He cried for them to believe it was all a terrible mistake.

In another part of the house, Hamish was being kept under a close watch. There was nothing he could do to help Harry. He heard him screaming, begging for mercy, crying for them not to hit him again. And again and again he screamed, each time Hamish wincing as if it was him being tortured. The minutes ticked away, and he heard nothing.

Harry's interrogators reluctantly agreed with Al to give Harry a break. Al saw they were enjoying their work. They left laughing at all those stupid, ignorant Jews who actually believed Harry was the Messiah. They were convinced he was a spy or in the service of a Prince of Arabia, but a Messiah they were sure he was not.

Harry awoke on fire from head to foot. No cot for him to lie on; the hard wooden floor had to do. No toilet; he had to relieve himself in the open. Too weak to move, he spilled his waste near where he sprawled.

Now that Harry's screaming had not been heard for some time, Hamish worried about what his captors were up to now. He worried about his daughter. He was as unable to help her as he was to help Harry. He felt guilty about Ashel. Maybe if he had done something different, Ashel would still be alive today.

"But what could I have done?" He tormented himself for the lack of anything better to do. "If it wasn't for me, the Wishnatski's wouldn't be mourning their son in jail!"

His self-hating struggle would have gone on, but for the sounds of another struggle taking place outside the room where he was being held prisoner.

He had little or no hope that he was going to get out of this jam in one piece, so it startled him when the door opened and in came Al dragging the guard by the scruff of the neck.

"Give me a hand," Al panted. "Hurry! Before someone comes along!"

They dragged the guard in.

"Is he dead?" Hamish kicked the door shut.

Al didn't care one way or the other as long as the man remained quiet. He dropped his end, and the guard's head fell to the floor with a thump.

"Hamish!" Al straightened up. "We don't have time for explanations. Let it suffice that I've had a change of heart."

"You need not explain to me. You're here—that's enough as far as I'm concerned." Without another word, he reached for the door and looked out cautiously. "We're in luck! All's clear! You know where they're keeping Harry?"

"Follow me!" Al led him to a staircase and they climbed two flights up. At the top of the stairs, Al stopped. He whispered to Hamish that he should wait where he was.

Peering around the corner, Hamish watched Al talking to a man that he recognized from before.

"Hi," said Al. "I've been told to relieve you."

"About time," the guard replied. "I was supposed to be relieved an hour ago."

As soon as he turned his back, Al reached inside his jacket and pulled out a gun, hitting the man as hard as he could on the back of the head. Without uttering a sound, he slipped into Al's waiting arms.

Hamish came quickly.

"Get the keys!" said Al. "There, in his pants pockets."

"Got 'em!" He fumbled with the lock. Finally, it clicked, and he pushed open the door.

There, lying in the middle of the room, eyes wide, aflame with fright was Harry. He held his hands out in front of himself in a futile attempt at protecting himself.

"No, don't! No more! Please! I'll admit to anything you want me to!"

Hamish knelt at his side. "Harry, it's me, Hamish! Al and I have come to take you away from here!"

"Is it really you?" Harry ran his fingertips down the side

155

of Hamish's face.

"It is." Harry allowed Hamish to take him by the armpits and lift him to his feet. Hamish almost vomited, looking at Harry's poor body.

"What have they done to you?" He saw on his chest and stomach were dozens of small cigarette burns. His back had been strapped till the skin blistered. Harry's legs were wobbly; he had to lean on Hamish to walk.

Al winced and shook his head. "I'm sorry," he said to Harry.

"Save your apologies for later," said Hamish anxiously. "Let's get going while we still can. We've made enough noise to alert the whole house."

There was but one way out, Al said. And that was the same way they had come.

Down the short hallway! So far so good! The tension was near the breaking point as they hurried down the stairs as quickly as Harry could go.

At the bottom of the stairs, the front door in sight, their good luck deserted them. There came the bad—hollering and shouting for them to stop, shooting their guns when they did not.

Al returned fire. Hamish pushed Harry behind the staircase. A bullet ripped into Al's shoulder, but before it did, he shot down two of their attackers.

The shooting was resounding. Al holding them off. He yelled for Hamish to reach into his coat pocket.

Hamish did and pulled out a small bundle of papers. "What's this?"

"They're the papers you and Harry will need to get out of the country. Go on! I've parked a car outside. The keys are in the ignition. Go on, I'll cover you!"

"No!" snapped Hamish. "What about you? I'm not leaving you behind too." He saw flashes of his daughter and Al's brother. He saw Donna and Irving moving before his eyes.

Al's shoulder was bleeding profusely.

156

"Our duty is to bring Harry home," said Al through clenched teeth. "As soon as you two are safely out of the house, I'll follow. Now go on, get the hell out of here!"

Hamish took hold of Harry. "Ready!" he said.

Al started firing rapidly.

Hamish screened Harry's body from harm with his own and made a mad dash for the front door. Out the door they came, ignoring the bullets whistling overhead.

Hamish pushed Harry in the car, slid in after, and found the ignition. The engine roared. He hesitated for a split second before pulling away, but Al didn't show in the doorway. He pushed the clutch down slowly. Still no show! He had no choice and sped away.

The problem now was: what to do? As soon as Hamish was sure that no one was following, he pulled into a side street to think.

Poor Harry. He hadn't said a word since Hamish found him in that awful house. He agreed with everything and went along without a single protest.

Hamish decided first things first. He would find them a motel where he could clean Harry up, get him a change of clothing, and maybe even give him a couple of hours of sleep before they tackled going to the airport.

"But no more!" He was firm with himself. He and Harry had but one slim chance of escaping the country, and that he was convinced they must take quickly before something else happened and their one chance in a million disappeared to no chance at all.

Hamish drove across the city and out to Long Island where he found an out-of-the-way motel a couple of miles away from the airport. He left Harry in the car while he checked in, all the time keeping an eagle's eye on him.

Harry lifted his head and stared. The world seemed to have gone mad with anger. The many sorrows that made up his life flashed through his mind.

Store after store of Jewish-owned businesses, delicatessens, liquor stores, ladies' apparel, their windows smashed and all ransacked.

He saw himself standing outside Temple Beth El, its walls defaced with German Swastikas. There at his feet, written in blood—"Dirty Jews." A little further on, he stopped and watched some children playing in the park. Over behind a tall clump of bushes, a gang of boys had this one little girl cornered.

"Hey, Jewy!" They taunted, flipping up her dress cruelly. "No, don't!" she cried.

"The little Jewy wants it, fellows!"

"No!"

One of the boys slapped her in the face. She screamed and ran, crying out for help.

The boys chased after, catching up with every few steps taken. They ran past a police officer, who chuckled his approval. They ran around a couple strolling along, taking their baby out for some fresh air. They caught up with the little girl, pounced, and knocked her down on the ground. They tore at her clothing, cruelly pinching her tiny breasts.

And when she regained consciousness, the whole world had disappeared. She was alone, taking on all the burden for what had happened.

"You're not alone," shouted Harry. "I'm here with you!" He reached out to her, but instead of taking hold of the little girl, he grabbed hold of Hamish's arm.

"It's all right," said Hamish, concerned. "Harry, it's okay. It's me. Everything will turn out fine. You'll see." And as gently as he could, he helped Harry out of the car and into the motel room. He laid him on the bed, took off his tattered clothes, and tenderly cleansed his wounds.

"What's happening?" Harry breathed unevenly and clasped his chest. "Don't think about anything." Hamish wiped a wet cloth over Harry's forehead. "Clear your mind, close your eyes, and try to get some sleep."

Out of Hamish's concern, the few joys Harry had known in his life washed over him, and he fell fast asleep in a few minutes.

A few hours later, he was awakened by Hamish. He sat up in bed, rubbing his eyes, swollen and red.

"You slept well, I see."

"I think so," he replied, wishing to himself that he could sleep forever. It was dark, and it was cool, and for once he wasn't afraid. Surely this must be the Kingdom of Heaven.

"While you were sleeping," said Hamish, "I bought you some new clothes." He laid them on the bed. "Hope they're the right size. Go on, try them on."

Soon after, Hamish laid out his plan of operation. "We'll leave the car here and take a taxi to the airport. I've made reservations for us on the next flight to Israel under our assumed names. You're Harry Jones. I've made it simple for you, Harry, so you wouldn't have any trouble remembering your new name. Remember, Harry, if anything goes wrong and by some chance we get separated, keep going, stay loose, and get on the plane. Don't talk to any strangers, don't ask for any favors. When you land in Israel, tell the security people at the airport who you are, and they will take good care of you. You understand?"

"I do," replied Harry, but just to make sure, Hamish made him repeat it over for him.

"Good! Let's get this show on the road."

A couple of blocks away from the motel, Hamish flagged down a yellow cab.

"Where to?" The driver reached over the back seat and opened the door.

"Kennedy Airport," replied Hamish.

"You hear the latest?" said the cabbie, pulling into the lane of traffic.

"No, what?"

"The Jews are going to get us all killed yet," he said angrily.

159

"I don't understand. What have they done now?" It sounded strange to Hamish to call Jews "they."

"In the Middle East, they're pushing the Arabs too far. This morning, for example, I heard that the Israelis raided a refugee camp and murdered dozens of women and children while their menfolk were working in the fields. They go too far! This Megiddo who the Jews say is their Messiah is another Hitler, leading the so-called Chosen People against the decent people of the world. He pushed the Arabs into a war that is going to drag us all down with them!"

"Oh..." was all Hamish could say.

Harry sank lower in the back seat, keeping his face hidden in his hands.

"I heard on the radio a couple of minutes ago that the police raided a house and arrested a gang of Jewish terrorists. They found a lot of weapons and plans to blow up the United Nations. Dirty Jews!"

He spit out the window; the gob got caught by the wind and blown in Harry's eye.

What could Hamish say? He said nothing. He watched the road speed by. He guessed that the Jews the cabbie spoke of were the very same who had held Harry and him captive.

He thought about his daughter.

"You hear about the police raiding a Jew's house up in White Plains?" He leaned forward, resting his elbows on the front seat.

"I might have. I'm really interested in the Jewish question. But these days, the police are locking so many Jews up that soon there isn't going to be any room left for the niggers." He laughed caustically.

They drove over the ramp that pointed to the terminals. Red, blue, green, yellow. "Who you flying?"

"T.W.A.," replied Hamish anxiously.

"If I had a say" - The driver went ceaselessly on as if he knew that each utterance drove a dagger into his passengers.

"We'd open the detention camps we had—and rightly, I might add—to use during the big war to intern Japs in this country. Now! We got to lock up the Jews where they can't hurt decent folks like us."

A shudder went up and down Hamish's back. He felt first cold, then hot all over.

"And if our dumb-ass politicians don't get the message, we citizens, the common everyday tax-paying, hard-working men, are gonna have to take matters into our own hands. We want to be protected! Our children…!"

The cab pulled over and stopped. "Here we are, T.W.A." He reached over the front seat. "That will be six bucks, please!"

Thankful they were out of the cab; they checked in with no hassles. Their seats were reserved and confirmed, first class, no smoking. Flight 458 to Jerusalem with one fueling stop in Athens. Gate twenty-one, down the blue corridor. Departure in seventeen minutes.

"Have a good flight and hurry!" said the reservations. "Your plane is already boarding."

The terminal was crowded with travelers coming and going to every conceivable destination. Hamish hurried Harry through the terminal, down the blue corridor, where they had to pass through a metal detection check point. With more than a little trepidation, Hamish let Harry go first.

No problem. He followed after with the same results. None.

It was a breeze. Harry was waiting on the other side for him. He greeted him with a smile, grasped him round the shoulders, and led him off.

"We're home free." Hamish glanced down at his wristwatch.

What words were to have fallen from Harry's lips were never spoken. He clung to Hamish. His heart, relieved, opened and sighed.

"You're doing fine," praised Hamish. "In a few minutes,

161

you'll be flying home."

"Hello," greeted the stewardess. "May I see your tickets, please?"

"This is the most exciting thing that has ever happened to me," Harry exclaimed, following behind Hamish as he searched for their seats. "I've never been up in a plane before."

For a split second there, Hamish thought he saw Harry smiling. He was mistaken.

They found their seats, and Hamish helped Harry buckle in. "The most exciting thing that has ever happened to you... Hmm...? After all we've been through? You're unbelievable, Harry!" He glanced again at his watch. The plane was scheduled to take off in less than five minutes. It was now or never. He had to make his mind up and quickly. Tick tock.

"What could go wrong?" He gave Harry a quick glance. "Like I said before, it's free sailing from here on out." What Hamish was worried about wasn't Harry anymore. It was his daughter Deborah weighing his conscience down.

Harry, his nose pressed up against the window, watched intently the workmen fiddling around the jet. He relaxed a bit. Maybe once in Israel, things would work out better.

"What could go wrong?" Hamish made up his mind. "Nothing!"

He kidded himself that Harry would make it alright from here on out on his own.

"Harry," Hamish got to his feet. "I gotta go to the bathroom, and I want to remind you not to leave your seat or talk to any strangers while I'm gone." He reached into his coat. "Here's your ticket and passport and a little money in case the stewardess comes while I'm gone."

"I have to go, too." Harry didn't want to be left alone.

"Not now," Hamish was thinking about more important matters. "You wait here for me to come back. They don't allow two to go to the bathroom at the same time. Okay?"

He didn't ask, and with no further thought about Harry,

he turned and left.

The roar of the engine filled Harry's ears. The jet shook and trembled and then started to roll. Harry, sitting in the window seat, leaned over the empty seat and peered down the aisle. Still no sign of Hamish. He hoped he wasn't sick.

The jet lunged! Harry's heart thumped. He wished Hamish was there with him for the big moment. He was a little bit frightened. Down the runway, faster and faster, the jet lifted up, up, up through the clear blue sky.

The plane leveled off; the fasten your seat belt light went blank.

"This is your Captain," a commanding voice bellowed over the loudspeaker. "We'll be flying at approximately thirty-eight thousand feet. The temperature outside the cabin is a cool twenty degrees below zero. Our estimated time of arrival in Athens will be four fifty-three Athens Time. On behalf of Trans World Airlines and all the crew, I wish you a comfortable and pleasant flight."

Harry poked his ears. He couldn't make out all of what the Captain was saying.

"Swallow!"

Harry looked up, and there was the stewardess smiling down at him. He blushed. She was beautiful. He wondered what she wanted.

"Swallow!"

"What?"

"Swallow," she repeated. "It will help you clear your ears."

He took her advice and swallowed a mouthful of saliva. It worked a bit. He swallowed again. A little bit better, his left ear was clear. He swallowed once more.

"There!" he exclaimed. "I can hear. Thank you."

"Can I get you something to drink?"

Harry remembered what Hamish had said about him talking to strangers. He shook his head no.

"Would you like some gum?"

"Noo..."

The stewardess moved on.

Harry wished to God that Hamish would come back. He had to go to the bathroom so bad that his back teeth were floating.

"What's keeping him?" He was getting anxious.

— CHAPTER SIXTEEN —

Short of breath, wheezing for air, the whole world had gone mad, squeezing the good earth for all she was worth. Sirens started blasting.

"A bomb!" someone hollered, picked up by someone else and carried frantically through the terminal. People screaming, running wild in all directions, tripping, and pushing over each other. It was every man for himself.

"Hold it!"

Hamish saw two airport security guards crouched and pointing their guns at him.

"Hold it!" They threatened to shoot.

He moved to his left. No good; more police were coming that way. He spun to his right. Panicking people blocking his way. Instinctively, he reached and pulled out his gun. Before he could fire a single shot, the police let loose a barrage of bullets. One creased his forehead. He slumped to his knees.

In a matter of seconds, the security people were all over him. They wrestled him down to the ground. He was kicked in the head and ribs numerous times. His hands were twisted behind his back and handcuffed. He was surrounded by dozens of security police, all pointing their guns at him. One of the officers, overwrought by the battle, slapped Hamish behind the head with the butt of his pistol. His head snapped forward, coming to rest on his chest. As they rushed him out of the airport, Hamish opened his eyes, and through the daze, he saw many people lying on the floor, crying out for someone to help them. Everyone was busy and had problems of their own. The passengers lifted their silken dresses and stepped over the mangled outstretched arms.

"Truly, this must be the end of the world," thought Hamish just before he blacked out.

***

Hamish had been gone for an awfully long time. Harry was getting more and more uptight. Maybe he was sick after all, maybe worse? Harry didn't know what he should do.

He gazed out the window. There was nothing to see, and nothing was beginning to bore him. The aisle was filled with passengers idling about. The stewardesses were not upset at them. He decided to give it a go and see what was keeping Hamish.

Walking carefully sideways, he heard someone say, "Hello!" A strange man seated below tugged at his arm. Harry pretended he didn't hear, pulled his arm away, and continued on.

At the back of the plane, the stewardesses were rushing about, with cokes and magazines, pillows and blankets for the passengers.

"Could you tell me where the restroom is?" he asked, talking over her head to the wall. He thought to himself that Hamish told him not to talk to strangers, but he just had to find out what was keeping him.

"At the other end of the cabin," replied the stewardess closest to Harry, her hands full of trays stacked back to her elbows. "Excuse me."

"What?"

"Excuse me, I have to get by." The veins in her hands popped out under the strain.

Down the aisle, she passed out dinner. Harry followed behind. He stopped when she did. She saw him and said nothing. She had learned from six years' experience that in a matter of hours she wouldn't remember that Harry ever existed. His face would blur with the thousands of others she had served. She gave out the last of the trays and stepped to one side, allowing Harry to glide past.

He brushed into her. A tingle went up his legs. Harry was brooding over Hamish. "I don't need her or anybody else, except him. Soon we'll be landing in Israel, and he promised that I would be happy there."

At the back of the plane The stewardess, at least, hadn't lied to him. There were two bathrooms on either side of the cabin. He knocked on the door to the left. No answer. He knocked again, and when no reply was forthcoming, he sneaked a look around the cabin to see if anyone was watching. When he was satisfied there wasn't, he opened the door. The stool was vacant.

He was therefore positive that Hamish was in the other one. "Hamish?" he knocked on the door.

"Hamish, answer me. You all right in there?"

No sooner had he asked than the jet tossed in the air, thunder roared over the engines, and lightning could be seen clearly attacking. One passenger had his mashed potatoes jammed up his nose, while a jumpy cup of coffee burned another one's balls. The stewardesses rushed up and down the aisle helping out where they could. The 'fasten your seat belt' sign flashed on, and over the intercom, the Captain informed them that they were passing through a storm and would everyone please remain calm and in their seats.

"There is no cause for worry."

The plane tossed from dark cloud to cloud, fell and rose with Harry's stomach going with it. He pounded on the restroom door.

The stewardess came running from the other end of the cabin.

"What's the problem?" she panted.

"Hamish...! He's in there and won't come out! Something must be terribly wrong! He won't answer me!"

"Look..." She had very little patience left with him. She pointed over his head. "There's no one in there. The occupancy light is off." She pushed open the door. The bathroom was empty.

"Then where is he?" Harry hollered. "He told me he was going to the bathroom. Where is he?" Harry began to break apart.

167

"Who?"

"Hamish!" He shrieked. "The man I came on board with!"

"The man you came on board with left," she tried to keep her cool. "He said he had forgotten a package on the terminal and never came back on board."

"Hamish…!" Harry went out of his mind, his body quivering, tears dripping into his gaping mouth.

"Let me give you a hand back to your seat!" The stewardess was really beginning to worry about him. "Don't worry. Your friend will probably catch the next flight." She took hold of his arm.

"Oh, noo… Hamish...!" Harry tore his arm away, knocking her down. Stepping on her to get over, he ran through the cabin screaming for Hamish.

Pandemonium broke out on Flight 458. The storm boiled, tossing the jet from current to current. The other passengers began to panic, yelling for somebody to do something.

"Stop that man!" One of the passengers screamed. "He's heading for the emergency exit!"

"He's going to jump!" another hysterically screamed. "Stop him!"

The passengers panicked, jumped up from their seats, and ran up the aisle, down the aisle, knocking into each other.

"Where do you think you're going?" Captain Bombgardner pushed his way through. "Get back to your seats!" He shoved and pushed.

"Everyone, listen!" he hollered. "Get back to your seats!" He wouldn't take no for an answer, and those who wouldn't or didn't hear him, he shoved back into the seats.

At the back of the second-class cabin, his hand on the latch, his face white, his tongue hanging out, chewed and bleeding, Harry threatened, "Don't come any closer! Get back, or I'll jump!"

The captain froze, almost tumbling over.

"Okay, okay! Take it easy!" He held an open hand out. "Nobody wants to hurt you, mister."

"What have you done to Hamish?"

"Who?"

"Tell me," Harry screamed. "Tell me or I'll jump!" He turned the latch a bit.

"Hold it!" Captain Bombgardner yelled. "You open that hatch, and you'll take everyone down with you!"

"I don't care! I want Hamish!"

"I don't know what you're talking about, but I assure you, we've done nothing to hurt your friend." He turned to the stewardess closest to him. "You know what he's talking about?"

"His friend," she replied. "Back in New York, his friend got off the plane and said he'd be right back. He never did come back. That's all I know, I swear it!"

Captain Bombgardner thought fast, and if Harry tried to open the hatch again, he'd…

Harry did, and before he knew what hit him, the Captain knocked him to the floor.

Harry fought like a madman possessed with the strength of a lion. He flung the Captain off and bounced up to his feet, only to be knocked down again by one of the passengers who was glad to be of help.

Along with a few other of the passengers, they held a furious Harry down. He was choking on his own blood, spitting it up in their faces, kicking, and flailing his legs.

"Hurry!" snapped Captain Bombgardner. Harry lunged forward and bit into his ear.

"You son of a bitch!" He hit him with all his might in the side of the head. "Give him a shot of that knockout drug. In the first aid kit—that should keep him quiet for a while."

The needle slipped into his vein, pushed with a certain amount of relief by the stewardess. Harry, in a few seconds, stopped kicking and fighting. Everything began to go round and round. He moaned, "Hamish!"

Flight 458 flew on through the storm. The stewardesses were kept busy emptying and replacing the bags that the airlines provide in case of airsickness. The cabin stank to high heaven; the gagging drowned out the roar of the jet engines. Harry was carried to the front of the cabin where the crew could keep an eye on him. On orders from the Captain, Harry was to be kept sedated for the rest of the flight. Captain Bombgardner radioed ahead to Athens and reported to the local police officials what had transpired on board. He requested that as soon as the plane landed, the police should come aboard and take the mentally deranged passenger into custody.

Hours later, they flew out of the storm and into a clear blue sky. The passengers relaxed, giggled, and bragged about their bravery during the calamity.

"If it wasn't for him, if it wasn't for her, if it wasn't for the stewardesses, how about the Captain, wasn't he wonderful?"

"But what about that lunatic? What the hell happened? Was he out of his mind? If he wanted to kill himself, who cares? What pisses me off is that he had to pick a place that threatened me and my family!"

The crew had orders to keep the other passengers away from Harry.

He could hear them talking about him, but he couldn't reply. Something was wrong with his tongue! He couldn't move it. He ordered his hand to wave for attention. It refused to respond to his direction. He tried his legs. They wouldn't budge.

"They must be in cahoots with all the others who are out to get me!" He wanted to cry, but he had no tears left.

With a good tailwind pushing them along, Flight 458 arrived forty-five minutes ahead of schedule. They were met by the Greek police as soon as they taxied to a stop. The door swung open. The police rushed in and wouldn't allow anyone to disembark until all had been questioned.

While the police investigated, the doctor examined Harry. The stewardess explained that all of a sudden, without any warning, he had gone berserk and had threatened to open the emergency door and jump.

The Captain explained to the police that if he had managed to open the door, they would not be here now to report what had happened.

"Why's your ear all swollen? Nasty looking," one of the officers asked.

"I got it," he rubbed his ear, "while struggling with him! He bit my ear!"

"Assault," quickly replied the officer in charge. "Disorderly conduct, attempted suicide. That should do for now. I believe we have sufficient cause to put..." He opened Harry's passport: "Mr. Jones into custody."

"That's what I wanted to hear, replied Captain Bombgardner with relief. "He's all yours, and I don't mind telling you that I'm happy as hell to wash my hands of him!"

The doctor, leaning over Harry, tending to his cuts and bruises, looked up.

"This man is in a state of shock," he said to the officer in charge. "And it's no wonder! His body is riddled with horrible cuts and bruises. Look here!" He opened Harry's shirt for all to see. "His chest is a mass of what I believe to be cigarette burns, while his back,"—he" pushed him to one "side—"looks like it's been strapped. His wounds are nasty, but most are superficial except for his tongue." He eased Harry onto his back and moved up to open his mouth.

"He bit his tongue off. By the way," he asked the Captain, "you wouldn't happen to know how this man came to be in this state?"

"No..." Captain Bombgardner wrinkled his lips.

"Too bad!" The doctor turned his attention back to Harry and allowed his mouth to fall shut.

"Hey, Captain, you wouldn't by any chance have picked

up the piece of his tongue he bit off, would you?"

"No…!" The thought disgusted him.

"Pity, I might have been able to sew it back together. Oh well! We'll never know, will we, Captain…?"

"I guess not."

"If I could make a suggestion," he said to the police.

"Go on."

"I think it is important to Mr. Jones that we take the time to look. We know it's in the cabin. It shouldn't take too long to find it."

The police agreed over the objections of the Captain, who argued he had a schedule to keep and didn't have the time for any nonsense. He was overruled, and a search was begun, with the passengers volunteering to help.

Harry didn't care if they found his tongue or not. He never wanted to talk to anyone again. He didn't care if he ever moved his arms again. He didn't! He was serious. They could take him anywhere they wanted. He wouldn't fight it. They could throw him in a deep, dark dungeon, put an iron mask over his head, and let his beard strangle him slowly to death. Even if he could, he would not cry out if they burned his eyes out with hot charcoals, tore the skin slowly off his bones, buried him up to his neck, poured molasses over his head, and let an army of red ants run in and out of his ears and nose, eating him alive from the inside out. He could not care less.

The passengers and crew were on their knees searching for the tiny tip of Harry's tongue. They looked under the seats and felt under the cushions. Twice they searched the floor thoroughly. They were about to give up.

"There!" one of the children exclaimed, pointing to the Captain's trousers. There sticking over the cuff was the tip of Harry's tongue.

Captain Bombgardner shook his foot disgustedly until it fell out. The doctor reached over, picked it up, and put it in his pocket.

"That does it!" he exclaimed. "Let's hurry. The sooner I get to sewing it back together, the better the chances of it sticking."

Harry didn't care. He was a disinterested onlooker.

The passengers disembarked from the rear of the jet. They congregated at the foot of the ramp, watching as Harry was carried on a stretcher off the front and placed in a waiting ambulance.

A few minutes later, the ambulance silently sped off and disappeared round the corner of the terminal building.

***

The same morning, just after dawn, the police in New York City were still interrogating Hamish.

"We know you're an Israeli agent. You've been identified as being with the fugitive leader Harry Megiddo on at least three different occasions. We know you know where he's hiding. We'll find him eventually, anyways, so you might as well come clean and make things easier on yourself."

Hamish, tired and beat from lack of sleep, his head splitting from the wound on his forehead, refused to answer their questions all night and in the morning was still holding out.

To any who happened to ever have had any business behind its formidable walls, the city jail was known as the Tombs. Hamish was taken from the interrogation room up to the cells on the top level. Shivering and shaking, senses weirded, willing to swear to God that he was descending into hell.

Row after row of Black men behind bars, reflecting light off their shiny white teeth into his eyes.

I'll tell you nothing! There's nothing you can do to make me. My people have seen the inside of hell before. You do not frighten me!"

"You're missing the point." One of his guards twisted his fingers cruelly. "Your people might have, but you ain't seen nothing yet!" His shrill laughter echoed off the damp thick walls.

He thought he heard someone shouting his name. It

sounded like a woman's voice. It couldn't be! He hadn't seen anyone but Black men. But yet…?"

Abruptly, he was jerked to a stop.

"Oh no!" he gasped. It was Deborah, his daughter.

"You sons of bitches!" He fought to break free, but it was a futile gesture in his weakened condition.

"Now we're getting somewhere," his tormentors laughed. "You two know each other? Hey?"

"My God!" Deborah cried. "What have they done to you?" She raised her fists but couldn't reach far enough through the bars to strike the men holding her father.

"You know this woman?" One of the interrogators reached through the bars, pushed Deborah's fist to the side, and grabbed her by the throat. He squeezed till she gagged. He squeezed still tighter till the hairs on the back of his hand stood up straight and tall.

"Noo…" Hamish groaned gutturally.

"Deborah's face turned blue. "You know her?"

"No…!" Hamish forced it through puckered lips.

Deborah passed out, her head slumped over the massive hand, which tightened and tightened its grip.

"Yes… Yes…!" cried Hamish, not able to risk holding out any longer. He was sure that the bastard would choke her to death. "Yes! For God sake! Stop it, you're killing her!" wildly flinging his head back and forth. "I'll tell you anything you want to know."

"Now, that's more like it." He let Deborah loose and let her head drop down on the hard, cold cement block floor. He leaned close to Hamish. His sour breath was nauseating.

"Now, I'll start over simple like. You know this girl?"

"Yes, yes. I've already admitted that! She's my daughter."

"Your daughter…" The other guard was staggered. Then he got mad. "Your daughter!" His voice dripped with anger.

"You wouldn't be putting us on, would you, bub?" He reached back between the bars and dragged Deborah by the hair.

"I'm telling you the truth," screamed Hamish. "She's my daughter, I swear it!"

"And you're both Israeli agents?" He started twisting her head.

Hamish thought her head would snap any second. "I am!" he cried out. "She's an innocent. She has nothing to do with any of this. You have to believe me!"

He let go of her head. "That's the attitude I like to hear. Cooperation."

"I want to call a lawyer!"

"A lawyer," his tormentors laughed hysterically. "The little man wants to call his lawyer! He's a comedian! All you Jews are the same, funny as hell!"

"But I'm not laughing, as you can see." His partner threatened. "You have no rights in this country, none whatsoever. Neither you or your daughter. You're Jews! You're both damn lucky that you're not dead! You can thank your lucky stars. Some people," he sneered, "would do terrible things to spies, and you're worse. You're both terrorist murderers!"

Hamish said nothing. He couldn't draw his eyes off his daughter. She hadn't moved since her head hit the floor; not a muscle quivered. From where he was standing, he couldn't make out whether she was breathing or not.

"Now," the guard lifted Hamish's head, "I want you to listen to me very carefully. You answer me truthfully, and you and your daughter will be well taken care of. Lie to me or refuse to answer, and I'll give her over to the niggers in the cell block for the night!"

Hamish hardly heard a word he was saying.

"She's dead! She's dead! Is she?" filled his mind and drove off any other considerations.

"We want to know where the other Jews are hiding."

"What… There aren't any others!"

175

"I won't repeat myself again! Where are Harry Megiddo and his followers hiding?"

Hamish could feel the sour breath on the back of his neck. It crawled over the goosebumps.

"She's dead!" he muttered. "You killed her, you sons of bitches!" he screamed.

"She's not dead, you fool. She's passed out." One blurred face said to the other to get some water and throw it over the girl.

But Hamish didn't hear. "She's dead!" filled his universe.

"You want to know where the Messiah is? You want to know?" He screamed hysterically for revenge. "It's too late," he horribly laughed, his features twisted with rage.

"I'll tell you!" he thundered. "It's too late by now for you to stop him!" Hamish was cold, empty inside. "You're right! My daughter and I were with Har Megiddo! We were assigned, along with others, to protect the Messiah till he finished his Lordly work here in America. Too late!" he laughed maniacally. "The Messiah was in this country to recruit as many of our people as he could to go to Israel and join the Legions of Megiddo!"

"Where's he hiding?"

"By now," Hamish, face tear-stained, "Har Megiddo is in Israel. By now, he has taken command of all Israeli armed forces. A curse on all the nations of the earth. Now you will pay for what you have done and are continuing to do to Jews. You'll pay."

"That's what you were doing at Kennedy! You were leaving, not coming. He got past us!"

"Yes...!" Hamish's teeth showed the fangs of a wounded animal. "Right through your slimy fingers. The Messiah slipped right through your security people and out of the country. Too late!" Hamish growled. "The Messiah is home with his people, and you, the whole world, who for so long hunted Jews, are no longer the hunter but the hunted now. The wrath of God through his spirit, Har Megiddo, spells doom for all of you."

"We're through with him!" One of the guards told the other to put him in the hole, where he could scream and holler till his lungs folded up.

"And her?"

"Give her to the niggers!"

As soon as the interrogators' superior got their report, he hung up the black phone and immediately reached for the blue.

"I got it."

"You sure?"

"I'm sure," he replied. "It's got to be Flight 458, Trans World Airlines."

"One fueling stop in Athens."

"Check."

His superior hung up the blue phone and eyed the red. He gave it considerable thought before reaching for it, and when he did, he did so with reluctance.

The order was given that Flight 458 Trans World to Jerusalem was to be brought down at any cost. The fugitive Harry Megiddo was on board, and he should be considered armed and dangerous.

The message was received a few minutes later at the control tower of Athens airport. The Greek government gave orders to hold Flight 458 on the ground.

The air controller shouted over the commotion around him that he couldn't hold the plane because it had already taken off fifteen minutes ago.

"Okay, okay! Hold your pants. I'll check her position right away!" He turned to check the radar screen. "She's gone!" he exclaimed.

"Take a look at this," he shouted to the other controller on duty.

"Disappeared! Flight 458 has disappeared from the screen. She must have gone down in the Mediterranean Sea!"

— CHAPTER SEVENTEEN —

But behold, the next morning a terrible piece of news swept through Israel, along with unseasonable rains and high winds, which knocked the olive crop off the branches to lie later rotting in the hot sun.

Mordecai, dripping wet, arrived at Yeshaayia's tent at the fringe of the desert on the outskirts of Jerusalem. He was excited—could barely contain himself. He was stopped by Rachel, who wouldn't let him out of the storm till he calmed down.

"I won't have you waking Father," she said angrily, pushing on his chest to keep him out. "Father hasn't had a minute of peace, hasn't caught a wink of sleep in almost a week! I won't have you disturbing him. If you'd like to come in, you'll have to keep your voice down!"

"I promise!" He held up his hand, his demeanor unmistakably excited.

"I won't stand for any more lies…!" For the first time in her memory, she locked eyes with Mordecai and held till he looked away.

Mordecai knew that Rachel knew that he had lied along with the Rabbi about the baby. He couldn't muster the fortitude to answer her innuendos.

He coughed. Rachel stepped aside and let him pass. She stared beyond him at the congregation of believers massed in the rain, waiting to see, to hear, maybe even to touch the Prophet Yeshaayia. The maimed and crippled, the diseased and blind were coming in an ever-increasing flow from the road running by yonder rise, from the desert, from cities and villages—all were gathering to see her father.

"How can you stay so calm?" Mordecai rubbed his hands vigorously.

"What…?" she replied, not feeling any of his sense of urgency. She was like a painted still life, standing motionless.

"What's the big deal now, Mordecai?" Her moment slipped by.

"It's dripping off everyone's lips. They're rushing out here expecting the Messiah to show up. The nation's been put on a high state of alert! Don't tell me you haven't heard?"

"And what's that we should know?" It was Yeshaayia awaking from a fitful sleep. "What is it?" He had a glint in his eyes.

"Oh, father…!" exasperated, Rachel squatted at his side. "I so wanted you to get some rest."

"Shhh…" he silenced her. "The Lord woke me, and what could I say: 'Come back when I've finished my beauty sleep?'"

He waved for Mordecai to come closer. "Now tell me. What are the people outside so excited and angry about?"

"He's alive!"

"Who?" Rachel asked.

"I told you before, Har Megiddo!"

"Har Megiddo! Har Megiddo!" She stammered, "How do you know for sure? Have you seen him?"

"No… But… He's…"

"For weeks there have been stories from every corner of Israel that he has been seen. What makes you and all the others so positive this time?"

Yeshaayia listened intently. He had a feeling this was why God woke him up.

"This time it is different," Mordecai replied. "I swear to you, I'm not lying this time. For the first time, we know for sure where Har Megiddo is at!"

"He's in the Holy Land! Finally, he has come," calmly said Yeshaayia.

"I knew it! I knew it! It has all not been for naught. I'm not crazy! I don't hear imagined voices. God has spoken to this putrid soul. He's here, thank God!" Yeshaayia closed his eyes, teetered, tottered.

Rachel leaned her father on her shoulder. "Not one

pillow for his comfort." Her eyes roamed the bare, empty tent.

Yeshaayia smiled wider than ever. He broke the scab open that had formed over the cut on his cheek. It bled.

"Don't excite yourself unnecessarily, Father. If the Messiah is truly here, he will come to see you before he visits anyone else." Rachel pressed a rag of burlap to his cheek, soon soaked through. "You mustn't," she chided, reminding him that the last time he broke open the cut, it had bled non-stop for two whole days. "You almost died," she cried.

"I will see his glory," trembled Yeshaayia. "God has promised me that I would live long enough to see his spirit working his miracle in the Holy Land. Don't be frightened, children!"

Mordecai was down on his knees, tears rolling down his face, swallowing the words he wanted to say.

"Yeshaayia," Mordecai choked up. "The news of the Messiah isn't all glad tidings. I don't know how to put it to you."

"Say it outright!" Rachel had very little patience with her husband. "Say it straight out for once in your life!"

"The path of Glory is sown with many blades of grass. If you walk lightly and have glad tidings in your heart for all of God's creation, you will pass over unharmed," said Yeshaayia, smiling and bleeding.

"Then, I'll tell you and ignore your feelings." Mordecai's pride was hurt by Rachel. "No fooling around! I won't throw any punches."

"What?" exploded Rachel.

"It is true that we know where Har Megiddo is, but so do our enemies."

"Where?" hollered Rachel. "Have pity on my father! Tell us what you think you know!"

"Har Megiddo was being flown from the United States to Israel when the plane he was a passenger on was hijacked by Arab terrorists."

"Oh no…!" gasped Rachel.

"No one promised that his bed would be made of anything but thorns," serenely said Yeshaayia.

"The terrorists have forced the plane down in the Sinai not too many hours from here. Only this morning an Egyptian fighter was shot down by one of our fighter pilots over the spot where he and one-hundred and fifty other passengers are being held captive for ransom."

"Oh no...!" gasped Rachel. "This is not the way it's supposed to be."

"It is the way," replied Yeshaayia. "It is the right way, if it is the way."

"All of Israel, Yeshaayia, is on a war footing. Our enemies are massing armies on our borders. I'm afraid it is only a matter of time before we must once again fight for the right to survive."

"I'm frightened!" Rachel bowed her head.

Yeshaayia said nothing and stared through the tent to the desert outside.

"Oh yes and more," said Mordecai madly. "The United States, our friends, have ordered their embassy to leave the country and return home immediately, breaking all diplomatic relations with Israel."

"Why?"

"They buckled under the pressure after we shot down that Egyptian fighter."

"The Lord weaves his web in mysterious ways, sometimes unfathomable to mortals."

"He certainly does!" Mordecai cracked his knuckles. "He has a half dozen nations outside of the Arab world sending not only armaments to our enemies but also troops."

"Why?"

"Who are you, me, you, or anyone to question God?"

"That is a question Jews have been asking themselves for as long as there have been Jews," said Mordecai. "I think Golda said it best when she said that other people hate us simply

181

because we won't go away. They kill us, send us into slavery, build gas chambers to do it more efficiently, but still we refuse to die! We survive! That is the sin!"

"And Har Megiddo?"

"He exists! We know that for sure! He's being held captive, stirring up an already boiling pot, and there are more than a few people who would like to see us boiled alive."

"How? Why? What has he done?" Rachel believed and was beside herself with grief.

"He's probably done nothing. That isn't where it's at. All over the world, Christians, Moslems, Communists have united together in their belief that he has committed hideous crimes against their God or the natural way of life. Their leaders tell their people that Har Megiddo is a monster leading an army of monstrous people. In the same breath, he is accused and convicted of committing dozens of crimes at dozens of different locations all at the same time. Our enemies are using him to destroy Israel for their own perverse reasons."

Mordecai paused barely long enough to catch a breath of air. He ranted on. "It's worse now than it was when the Nazis were in power in Europe. Especially in America!"

"No!"

"Yes, and I've heard that our people are frantically trying to smuggle as many Jews as they can out of the United States before it's too late. The Americans have gone crazy, out of their heads. They've lost their marbles and have started to kick Jews around. Using Har Megiddo as an excuse, as if they needed one to do what has been buried in their natures. A law has been passed and was signed by their President to open the detention camps last used to intern Japanese Americans. They're being readied to house Jewish Americans."

"Oh..." wept Rachel. "Is this what you've been waiting for all these years?" she said to her father, sobbing. "Is this what God's Messiah brings as a gift to the Chosen People? Maybe we'd all be better off today if we had followed the way of the late great Rabbi Tzadikovich?"

"We follow his way," Yeshaayia replied. "There is but one path, and it's as wide as the universe. Who knows, who can fathom what the Lord has strewn along the roadway? He has his design, of which we're all a part, for all time to come, for all time that has passed, for all time being. We are what we are, whether we like it or not."

"If these disasters have produced any good," Mordecai said, "our people have put aside their petty disagreements in the face of any enemy whose threat has grown as tall as Goliath."

"I guess our enemies didn't think that would be the results of their threats," replied Rachel, better composed.

"They are too of the flesh," replied Yeshaayia. "Like you and I, think of Rabbi Tzadikovich, bless his soul. Like the air, which is God's flesh, we all have our parts to play."

"You know?" exclaimed Mordecai.

"I am an ignorant man," Yeshaayia replied. "That I know. I know I can neither read nor write. I know that I am old and sick. I understand that soon I will die. What would you have me say, Mordecai, that I understand?"

"He does! Look at his face! He gives himself away," Mordecai bounced up on his feet. He pointed, "Look at your father, Rachel. He knows what this is all coming to!"

Yeshaayia didn't answer, his smile gave nothing and everything away.

***

Outside the Knesset, hundreds of outraged religious fanatics chanted their demand that the Prime Minister step aside and allow Har Megiddo to take the throne of David. "It has been written so. Let the government follow the Lord's teachings!" they shouted. "Har Megiddo! Har Megiddo!" They rallied round the Messiah.

A hush fell over the world, everyone holding their breath. Unbelievable. Truly remarkable. Staggered everyone watching. From coast to coast in the United States, across the Atlantic to Europe, and across the Pacific to Asia, Israel's

183

distorted, enraged face was carried by the miracle of television: Har Megiddo, leading hordes of Jews against the sovereign nations of the world.

Riots broke out in many countries. Jews were dragged from their beds in the middle of the night, beaten by mobs, encouraged by their leaders. The Vatican called for a holy war and urged all Christian nations to gather their arms to free the birthplace of Christ. From Moscow, the Russians rushed weapons to the Arab nations and urged them to fight to the death against the Zionist menace. It was confirmed that the Soviets were airlifting soldiers into Egypt and Syria.

The United States has demanded that the government of Israel return to the 1948 boundaries and that they turn over the criminal Har Megiddo to stand trial for his crimes in the country of his birth.

Inside the Knesset, the Prime Minister was addressing himself to these pressures. "It has been confirmed by our operatives in the United States that Har Megiddo is on the hijacked jet. Taken hostage with him are another one hundred and fifty Jews."

"What ransom do the terrorists ask of us?" a member of the opposition party questioned.

"They say they will kill Har Megiddo and everyone else on board unless..." He deepened his voice. "Unless we surrender Israel to them."

"Never...!"

"Maniac...!"

"They demand the impossible!" roared the assembly.

"Anticipating your response," replied the Prime Minister, "I have ordered a full military alert. I have also ordered units of the Israeli armed forces into the contested area of the hijacked plane to attempt a rescue. It's a matter of hours before I can report to you the outcome of the operation."

"And what if our enemies reach the plane first?"

"I have given orders that under no circumstances will

Har Megiddo and the others be allowed to be taken prisoner."

Then he turned his attention to the other nations of the world. He pointed out that Israel's neighbors, with military support from many nations, were at this very moment gathering to attack Israel. He warned all nations that Israel would use any means at her disposal to protect her integrity from invading armies.

He opened his fist. "I would like to speak to all peoples, Jews, Christians, Communists, about the one called Har Megiddo." His voice pitched lower by a couple of octaves.

"At this very moment belligerent forces from many countries are converging on a small speck in the desert. I warn all nations that we are speeding towards a calamity of the greatest proportions and that any attempt to seize the plane and its passengers will be construed as an act of aggression against the State of Israel. It will be met and repulsed by our armed forces. I warn all nations to stay out of the area. I repeat! I warn all nations to stay out of the area! There can be no winners in this war," he said in a deadly serious voice. "Israel is willing to meet with any government to talk of the end of all hostilities and grievances that other peoples' feel towards our nation, but I must warn them, in the strongest language possible, and make it clear to all nations, big and small, that Israel is willing to use any means necessary to guarantee the safety of her citizens."

He breathed deeply, let his breath out slowly, and loosened his shirt collar. He pointed out that Israel was surrounded by armies of enemies. He made a plea for unity, to end all differences.

"We must bind our wounds. We must put our differences aside. We must unite against our common enemies who are once again banging at our door. Individually," he held up his hand, "these fingers are nothing; we are nothing!" He closed his hand into a fist. "But together, we are a power to behold!"

— CHAPTER EIGHTEEN —

Thunderbolts crackling at each other, morbidly laughing at the people down below. In the middle of nowhere, on a windy, rainy, cold night, the hostages huddled together in the back of the plane. It was incredible! Grotesque! The desert, breaking out in rashes, echoing across the expanse, loud, terrifying explosions. A light bulb burst and burst without going out, blinding anyone who happened to be looking out the window. Over their heads, dogfighting it out, the terrorists fired at unidentifiable jet fighters and helicopters. Inside the plane, the hijackers were getting dangerously impatient. "Which one of you is he?" A terrorist stuck the muzzle of his rifle up the nose of a woman holding tightly on to her baby.

"Whooo..." trembled from her dry, swollen lips. She clutched her child tighter, shifting her body between the baby and the hijackers.

He grabbed the child out of her arms. The baby screamed as her hands were forced behind her back.

"Point him out! Har Megiddo!" He forced the child's elbows to touch. She screamed!

Her mother begged. "I don't know! I don't know! Leave my baby alone!" She cried, clutching his pants leg.

He kicked her away. "Har Megiddo? Which one!"

None of the passengers said anything. They were stunned. Flaming with anger, "You have till morning to turn your Saviour over to us. If not, thereafter on the quarter hour, one of you will be shot! Starting with the children!" He picked the little girl up and threw her over his shoulder and barged out of the cabin. Fighting with all at their disposal to save Har Megiddo and the rest of the hostages were the very best Israel had to offer. They weren't making much headway, but at least they could report back that the enemy wasn't either. Their losses were high in men and equipment, but the enemy was paying three to one. They fought on with no rest, praying that they could fight their way in before it was too late.

***

The remainder of the night, the same goings-on continued, only worse. It was more horrible for the hostages than they could have ever imagined in their wildest dreams. They were given no food or water; their blankets were taken away. It was almost morning, and still Har Megiddo hadn't stepped forward.

"For God's sakes! What kind of man are you? They'll kill my baby if you don't give yourself up!"

No one stirred a muscle. They stared at each other, barely chancing a breath, saying with a look, "It's not me. If not me, then who?" They scoped each other out.

"The sun will soon be showing itself," said Abe, who was running away from America with his wife and five children. "I never thought that the sun's appearance would cause me distress, but it does, and we have to come to some kind of decision before the Arabs kill all our children!"

"What...? What can we do against them? They have all the guns! We have only our bare hands!" An argument ensued.

"I have an idea," shouted Abe over the commotion. "It is not one I would guess everyone will like. But...it's an idea."

"Let's hear it."

"I say we're wasting what precious little time we have left in waiting for this Har Megiddo to step forward. If he's among us, of which I have my doubts, obviously if he hasn't stepped forward yet, he has no intention of doing so."

"So what are you suggesting?"

"I'm suggesting," he spoke rapidly, "that all the men draw lots. The winner or loser, take your choice, takes Har Megiddo's place and gives himself over to the Arabs."

"You're kidding!"

"No! I won't let my husband do it!"

"No, I agree!"

They hummed and hawed, bickered almost to the point of fisticuffs.

Above the din of war and noise, Abe yelled, "We don't have much time left. Why don't we put it to a vote? What do you say?"

They said they'd argue some more, but time was a thing that wouldn't stand still. So, after a few more minutes, when the sun's rays were unmistakably heading their way, they agreed to put Abe's plan to a vote.

Abe asked for all those who agreed with his plan to raise their hands. He counted. "Very good. Now let me see a show of hands against." He counted.

"It's decided," announced Abe. "We all agree then on what's to be done." He saw their faces, scared and drawn. "Are there any among us who wish to be left out of the drawing?"

At that moment, if an angel descended from heaven and said she would grant one wish, most of the hostages would have flown with their families to a place of safety. Herbie, who led the descent, spoke for all:

"Good friends! We are good friends, you know, thrown here together against our wills to be used as pawns in a deadly game. We must play. Make our move—and if still no one has a better idea than Abe, I think there is no need for any more discussion."

"Please proceed," he nodded to Abe.

"Very good." Abe kept his eyes glued to the strips of cloth he tore, all long with one short.

Women and children and friends made during the experience, crossing their fingers behind their backs, saying their prayers under their breaths, prayed that their loved ones wouldn't pick the short cloth.

One by one, they took their turns and then stepped to the side to watch.

Along came the turn of Murray, a boy whose pimples still covered his face and shoulders. His mother protested that her son wasn't even fourteen yet.

"But mother," he calmly said. "I am a man. You said so yourself when I was Bar Mitzvahed."

He was adamant, and before his mother could stop him, he put an end to the argument by reaching into the hat.

"Oh no...!" she screamed. There, dangling from Murray's hand, was the short cloth. She grabbed the hat from Abe and searched for a shorter piece. There was none!

"Noo...!"

Murray was white. It hadn't gotten through to him yet that he was the chosen one. He heard, far off in the distance, his mother pleading for mercy.

"For who? For what?" He couldn't make it out. It was decided. He was to die so they all might live. He didn't really believe that anyone would kill him.

***

The stupefying effect of the drug wore off Harry slowly but finally dissipated. Why then could he barely move a muscle? Because he was strapped to his bed in a hospital with bars for windows and a solid steel door. No one cared in the whole wide world. Nobody! No one! Not a single solitary soul! How many times had he trusted others, and they had let him down. He hated the sounds and sights of people. He wished with all his might that God would strike him dead, and when God didn't, he held his breath thinking he would suffocate himself. His face turned red, his cheeks sucked in, his eyeballs bulged, he turned blue, and passed out.

And when he opened his eyes again, he knew immediately that he wasn't dead. There, bending over him, was a very human, very fat man, sneering down at him.

"Mr. Jones," the man's breath was foul. "Mr. Harry Jones?" Harry couldn't help it. His lungs screamed for a fresh breath of air. He breathed deeply, sucking in the garbage breath. He choked. That woke him up with a start.

"Good!" the fat man exclaimed. "I'm glad you're finally

awake. I can't be kept waiting. You know, of course, that I'm a very busy person. My name's Mr. Ashworth, and if you haven't surmised it yet, I'm your representative from the American Embassy."

"Huh...?" His tongue throbbed; he noticed for the first time. "It pains!" he exclaimed to himself.

"No sense in playing coy with me, Mr. Jones. You're in big trouble. You know that the Greek government has charged you with very serious crimes. If you don't want the help of your government, tell me, and I'll go about my business."

"Huh...?"

"Now, come on, Mr. Jones! How do you want it?"

"Mr. Jones?" Harry winced as the words rubbed over the sensitive tip of his tongue. Honestly, Harry hadn't the faintest idea what Mr. Ashworth was talking about.

"Mr. Jones...?" He pushed the words out from his throat, throwing them over the sensitive portion of his tongue. That was better.

"Yes, and there's no sense in denying who you are. I have your passport right here."

He opened it, and there was Harry staring him in the face.

"Mr. Jones, it says so right here." He showed it to him.

Harry saw. It sure was him, all right. There wasn't any use in lying. "That's my picture," he replied. "But... but... my name isn't Jones! It's Megiddo, Harry Megiddo," he announced without a care.

Ashworth was staggered. He belched. "I knew I shouldn't have hurried my dinner to come up and see if I could help you. My wife is right. I'm too soft. There's no gratitude left in the world anymore. Please, Mr. Jones. I'm in no mood for jokes. You'd better come clean. The truth... I warn you, or you'll find yourself locked up for the next ten years in a Greek mental hospital!"

"I'm telling you the truth," replied Harry, forgetting the pain in his tongue, thinking that he didn't care what happened to him. So, he told Mr. Ashworth everything that had happened that he could remember: names, places, and dates. He spoke so vividly and clearly, with such passion and tragedy, that when he was finished, the embassy man believed that he was telling the truth.

"Guard!" he hollered.

"Guard!" He banged on the steel door. "Guard, let me out of here!"

The guard opened the door. Without another word, he brushed past, and without looking back, he rushed out of the hospital, huffing and puffing. He drove to the Embassy as fast as he could.

"Har Megiddo not in hijacked plane. In a hospital prison ward in Athens!" He sent the message "Urgent" to the United States State Department.

***

Too late...! The message was lost under the pile of confusion caused by the Arabs and their allies when they launched an all-out assault on Israel.

The streets of Jerusalem were filled with the youngest and oldest Judeans. In-between ages were up at the front, fighting back an enemy thrusting in on Israel.

Their faces were somber. Children with parents dead or dying were directing traffic. Grandparents crying for their sons and daughters were staffing the hospitals, listening to the news reports that their army was being pushed back on every front.

From Lebanon, Palestinian and left-wing Lebanese, along with soldiers from Iraq and Cuba, drove into Israel, meeting savage opposition. The commander of the region urgently wired Jerusalem that the battle was bloody. They were slowly retreating. More men and support were urgently needed.

At the same time, the Egyptians had repulsed the first counterattack in the Sinai and were pushing the Israelis back. It was reported to military headquarters that it was only a matter of hours before the Egyptians overran the position where the hijacked plane was.

Israeli forces on the Golan Heights were retreating in the face of a massive Russian and Syrian tank assault. The Israeli commander on the Northern Front told his superiors that he wasn't sure his forces could hold out for much longer.

An hour later, with fortunes on all fronts worsening, the Prime Minister held a crisis session of his cabinet. He reported that the Americans had flatly turned down his request that all hostilities end and that all concerned parties meet in a mutually acceptable location to discuss a peace plan.

The reply came from the Secretary of State. He stated his government's position that it stood by its public pronouncements, that the United States' clear and unwavering policy was the unconditional surrender of the State of Israel.

The defense minister was the first to digest the news. He warned that this was the end of the Third Temple.

"Har Megiddo or not, our enemies are about to drive us into the sea! They'll accept no other conclusion. They mean to destroy us once and for all!"

The Prime Minister heard clearly the sounds of battle coming closer. Thereupon, he gave the order to activate Israel's Doomsday weapons!

"How did it all come to this?" He pondered over the march of fateful events that had overwhelmed his powers to cope.

"I warned them!"

***

It was more than an hour after the sun had risen, and still the terrorists hadn't come to claim Har Megiddo. The fighting outside had become vicious. If the bombing and the long-range artillery came one step closer, they would never know what hit them.

The hostages wanted to be brave. With all their hearts, they tried mustering their courage in an effort to tell Murray not to go out and take the place of Har Megiddo.

A terrorist swaggered down the aisle towards them.

Abe was sitting next to Murray. 'Truly…!' thought Abe, 'this boy is the Messiah if he sacrifices his life up for ours.'

The Arab stopped in front of him. "Har Megiddo?"

Two more terrorists came into the cabin, machine guns in hand, their eyes sunken deep into their skulls, determined to deal harshly, staring coldly through the hostages as if their existence meant little or nothing to them.

"Har Megiddo!"

The terrorist standing over Abe motioned with his gun out the window to his comrades, who were sticking a dagger into the throat of the small child taken earlier.

Out of the corner of his vision, Abe kept a close eye on Murray.

"Har Megiddo…!"

There was no way Murray could figure out how to get out of his lot. Guilt morally lifted him to his feet.

Abe couldn't allow the young man to go through with it. He put a restraining hand on his shoulder.

"I'm the one you're looking for. I'm Har Megiddo!" he exclaimed.

His wife screamed, "No! He's not Har Megiddo! He's Abe, my husband. These are his children. Tell them, children, that this man is your father!"

"No…!" snapped Abe before his children could utter a reply.

"I'm the one you're looking for!" He met the eyes of the terrorist. "Don't listen to that woman! I've never laid eyes on her before. She and her children only say what they do to protect their Messiah."

Two of the terrorists grabbed Abe immediately.

"No…!" Murray stepped forward. "I'm Har Megiddo!" he hollered. "Let him go! I'm the one you're looking for!" he pleaded.

193

"No, I am!" Another hostage sprang to his feet. "I am he!"

Then another.

"No, me...!"

"Me...!"

Every hostage, male and female, all the children old enough to understand, were on their feet, shouting and hollering that they were the Messiah.

The terrorist in charge ordered his comrades to get Abe out of the plane.

'Maybe everyone is the Messiah,' Abe thought. Never in his life had he felt closer to so many people.

He hadn't been pushed a dozen steps when the sounds of machine gun fire burst in his ears. He jerked his head around, and there was the lone hijacker shooting down the hostages—men, women, and children—in cold blood.

Abe's piercing lamentation shook his captors. He broke their hold and, with the strength of a madman, threw them aside, knocking them out.

He rushed to the back of the plane and jumped on the murderer's back. Abe beat him to the ground, kicked him again and again, and punched his head till it split open.

Up to his ankles in a pool of blood, Abe bent low and searched the pile of twitching corpses for anyone alive. He found his wife and cried. She was dead! Under her were their children, their bodies twitching, but the breath of life had ceased to flow. He cried, "They're all dead!" He pulled his hair out by the roots.

His senses gave out. He was caked from head to toe in the blood of his loved ones. Abe fled out of the plane, tripping and stumbling, screaming, not caring whether the bullets flying by his head killed him or not. He tore through the Arab lines, their bullets chasing after him into the desert, miraculously escaping deep into God's kiln.

**

There was another who was deep into the Lord's furnace.

194

Yeshaayia Gurevich had left his daughter and son-in-law soon after he was told Har Megiddo was in the desert. He left with no water to quench his thirst. His lips were swollen after many hours under the boiling sun. He wore no sandals, so his feet were scorched to the bone. He had no hat to cover his head; his brain was smoldering, squeezed dry by God's handiwork.

"Who...? Who's that...?" Yeshaayia sputtered from swollen lips. He stared to the left, then to the right. He turned around, and out of the nothing, riding on a white horse, was Har Megiddo, carrying the standard of David.

"I am Har Megiddo...!" cried Abe, running towards Yeshaayia. "I am the Messiah!" He flailed his blood-soaked limbs.

"Oh God!" Yeshaayia prostrated himself.

"Oh God! You have kept your word to this poor old soul. You have let me live long enough to see your Spirit!"

"A thousand years!" Abe came running at Yeshaayia. "Two thousand! No, three! Four, yes... forever and all time."

Yeshaayia saw Har Megiddo entering Jerusalem, with thousands of people lining the streets. He saw him taking the throne of David. He saw a thousand years of peace gracing the Holy Land.

Abe took Yeshaayia by the hands and raised him off the ground. They danced round and round.

"I do declare I am the Messiah. I'm the one you have been waiting for."

"And wherever you shall go?" Yeshaayia was aglow. He never in his wildest moments ever thought it possible to be so happy.

"Children will scatter flowers underfoot."

"And I will step so gently as not to hurt their fragile petals."

"And I will gather them after you."

"And I shall make a sweet nectar."

"And I will serve your children your ambrosia."

"And all the world will dwell in God's glory!"

The very earth under their feet shook and trembled. The desert sands shifted before their eyes. Above their heads, the sky split open into pieces and began falling to earth. From across the desert, fingers of fire spread out. Spectacular!

— EPILOGUE —

What was the Middle East ceased to exist, only the wind billowing fire and a rain of atomic particles that dared enter this land any longer. The effect rippled round the globe, shaking the planet at its very axis. What was left was washed over by tidal wave after tidal wave, killing untold hundreds of thousands of people, changing the landscape of the world in a matter of hours.

Har Megiddo? Who knows if he actually existed? How much of his life was truth? How much fiction? Who cared if the truth was less than the fiction? If the fiction was more real, then what actually took place? There must have been a reason for it because Har Megiddo became more than reality to all those who knew him—and much more to the scores of millions that would know him only through the impact his life had on legions of nameless mortals.

In the days that followed after the destruction of the Third Temple, the mere mention of Har Megiddo's name brought reverent fear to the hearts of humankind.

Stories were passed from mouth to mouth, stretching into legend, then written as gospel into a third generation of Holy Bibles, that Har Megiddo was the Son of God and that the difference between him and his older brother Christ was that Har Megiddo was sent by his Father to manipulate humankind into bearing the guilt for having trampled God's garden.

As a warning to the survivors of Armageddon to begin living in accordance with God's commandments, the followers of Megiddo told how the Messiah had survived, his bonds broken, and as the day concluded, he had dug himself out from under the rubble, and the course of destiny had struck out once again.

Traveling alone, destruction and misery wherever he looked. He set out to leave the city as quickly as possible. He lengthened his step, eating up the road.

Days went by. Oil ceased flowing. Highways were soon

197

clogged with rusting automobiles. Factories closed, and power plants shut down. Central authority gave way to anarchy, sidewalks to grass, and forests to animals. The cities, plagued with disease, were abandoned in a frenzy.

The Messiah had a destination in mind but no idea how to go about finding its location. How long did he search for his vision? Days? Months? Years? Steadfastly, he roamed from barren field to field, the distance not measured in acres, the mountains not measured in feet; or sometimes by boat, he crossed from muddy shore to shore, not to be measured in fathoms. It is a heartbeat.

He witnessed farmers banding together, protecting their livestock and woodlands from scavenging city dwellers.

"We are starving! We are cold!" They threatened to take what they needed.

The farmers, taking the city people at their words, shot them dead where they were standing. From his hiding place behind a stone boulder, Har Megiddo saw the farmers feed the dead carcasses to their animals.

"For sure this isn't what I'm looking for." And as soon as it was dark, he continued on.

Keeping off the highways and byways because of the gangs of marauders who would cut your throat for the flesh on your bones, he couldn't remember how long ago it was, but it was soon after he had left the crumbling rubble of the city behind him. He saw on the road a gang of cut-throats who waylaid a fat man and tied him to a tree. They forced his family to watch as they sliced him in chunks and fought over the lean cuts.

Keeping a safe distance away from towns and villages, whose dwellers proved time and again that they couldn't be trusted.

"Are you hungry…? Are you thirsty...? How would you like to sleep on a soft feather bed tonight?" They dangled in front of the unwary, tantalizing them through the barricades, where they were at once pounced on and made into slaves.

He saw women whose worth to men plummeted to any beauty less than spectacular; the women were killed for their meat, but many survived and banded together in the mountains, and woe to any man who strayed into the valleys between. The vision had happened; the Messiah was sure. It was a miracle, but where was his all-consuming thought.   He closed his eyes to meditate and find the answer. But sleep came and took him along. The next morning, a continuous downpour with strong winds at his back drove him on. The wind dried his eyes till it hurt to look. He wanted to speak, but the wind put a hand over his mouth.

"Be still," he was told.

All day Harry skimmed over the ground wrapped in the muscle-bound arms of the wind. Towards evening the wind died down, opened its arms, and let him slip to the ground.

While he slept, flesh, soul, and mind united, and a woman emerged from his ribs to keep him company.

When he awoke, he found himself lying in a bed in a strange little cabin. Startled, he sat up. He was gently restrained by soft hands.

"Who...? Who are you?" he exclaimed, his mouth gaping open at the comely woman sitting by his side.

"I am Rebecca," she replied. "Lean back," she stroked his face.

"You have been through much. Here." She held a bowl of hot lentil soup under his chin. "Go on, drink it. It will help you regain your strength." She scooped the soup up with a large wooden ladle.

"Open up." She knocked on his lips.

"Who are you?" He asked between swallows. "How'd I get here?" The soup felt good settling into his empty stomach.

Rebecca laughed, took the bowl away, and fetched him some more. "I see there's nothing wrong with your appetite. You'll be as good as new in a few days, thank God!"

"You really mean that?"

"I do," Rebecca smiled.

"Really?"

"Really." She looked on him with unmistakable affection.

"How did I get here?" he asked again, guzzling the second bowl of soup down greedily.

"I found you a little way from the cabin," replied Rebecca. "At first, I believed you were dead, but when I came closer, I saw that you were still breathing and carried you here."

"You did?"

"On my shoulders. I'm a lot stronger than I look."

"Thank you," Megiddo looked out the window, the mountains were up close. He remembered the gruesome stories about the Mountain Women and what they did to the men they captured.

"What do you intend doing with me?" He asked, too tired to be anything more than resigned to his fate, whatever it might be.

"Have no fear," Rebecca wiped his chin. "I will not hurt you. I'm bursting inside with life, and I need you."

Harry's attention was glued to the snow-capped peaks dwarfing the cabin. Many small dots bobbed against the backdrop of white, moving towards the house.

"You need never fear again," Rebecca reassured him. "The others know you are here and need you as much as I. They come to see you now. Have no fear in your heart. Here, neither man nor beast shall harm you."

***

In the house of Rebecca, the Messiah became a farmer, sowing fields of wombs. From high on top of the mountain and deep within the valley, women came in droves and competed to see who could give birth to the most. The years flew by, and the sons and daughters of Megiddo multiplied and resembled him. In the morning, after seeing the last of the women out for the day, Harry stood amazed at all God's creation, where the Lord had placed the orchards, vineyards, and mountains, all refreshing friends at his doorstep for him to commune with as one.

After a light breakfast fixed by Rebecca, he left for the open fields, surrounded by wildflowers. Their sweet fragrances filled his nostrils. Wild animals, having no fear of this man, tumbled playfully just out of his way. Bending to hand an acorn to a squirrel, he saw Rebecca between his legs, striding in the tall grass towards him.

"Father," she called gayly. All the women and children called him father. When they had first started, he couldn't remember. It seemed to always be his name.

Hand in hand, they sat down on the hilltop and surveyed all that was before them.

"Have the years been good to you?" Rebecca looked at this man, the only man she had really known.

"Have they been good years?" repeated Har Megiddo. "I can no longer remember a life before I came to this incredibly wondrous valley. Earlier, I tried counting the number of children we've had together."

"They're as numerous as the animals in the forest."

"Not quite," he laughed. "But almost!" He was proud of his virility. "And you, Rebecca, you have borne more fruit than any other woman in the valley."

She blushed.

"Don't be modest," he teased. "I have never told you for fear of hurting the others' feelings, but you, Rebecca, have always been and always will be my favorite."

"Have you noticed how the children grow?" replied Rebecca. The oldest are nearly full gown men and women. Have you seen how they look at each other?"

"I have seen," he replied. "I know it shouldn't, but it hurts me."

"Soon the children will be wanting to go off and start families of their own."

"I know."

"You sound sad."

"Oh no, dearest. That is how it should be. I am not sad, not exactly, anyways. For the first time since I came to this valley, and you promised me that I would never fear man or beast again, I fear! Not for myself, mind you, but for the children. What will become of my sons and daughters once they leave the valley? And they will leave! I am as sure of that as I am sure that one day I will die."

"I know not what will become of your children, Father, but it distresses me to hear you speaking of your death."

"I have been sitting here trying to remember what it was like in the outside world, and try as I may, I cannot."

"Why bother?"

"So I might prepare the children. We have heard stories from the occasional traveler who stumbled into our valley, stories of the tumult and chaos going on in the world. I fear for the children!" He bowed his head and cried.

"Dear Father," she stroked. "Be joyous. Do not think of what hasn't passed yet. See...!" She pointed. "Your seed still bears life." "And where Har Megiddo tears fell to the ground, flowers sprung up in full bloom."

***

Har Megiddo spent most of his afternoons now daydreaming under the almond tree, his snow-white beard waving in the air to the deer and antelope frolicking in yonder field. It had been a dazzling day earlier that morning, but it had darkened by afternoon, puffy grey clouds drifting overhead, and a light drizzle had begun to fall. Rebecca sat at his feet, busy knitting him a sweater for the winter. Rebecca saw him grow pale.

"Father," she said, stroking the insides of his thighs, "come into the house before you catch a chill in your bones."

"That's the problem," he replied. "I am old, and the young girls no longer flock to lie by me. My seed spurts now in memories. I spend my nights dreaming of what once was," he sighed. "It is nice but not as nice as it used to be." He shook his head tiredly. "Most of the children have left the valley and have made their homes in the outside world. I heard a rumor floating about that one of the children of Jack, a direct descendant of ours, has raised an army and set out to put the world right. I don't know anymore, Rebecca..."

"It seems to me that I've heard that somewhere before..."

Rebecca felt him shivering all over.

"Father! Please, please come into the house before you catch your death."

Hearing footsteps in the yard, he opened his eyes. It was the children.

"Not now!" He heard Rebecca telling them to come back later.

"No," he said, and with some great effort, he raised himself erect.

"The children come with their mothers to speak to their father. What is it, beloveds?"

"Oh, Father!" one of the children stepped forward. "I am the oldest of your children living in the valley, and I have been chosen to speak for all."

"Yes...go on." He leaned on Rebecca for support. "You weren't taught to be afraid to speak your mind."

"I made the choice over a year ago to tackle the long trek out of the valley."

"I have never stopped anyone from leaving. Not physically, at least." He looked to Rebecca for an answer. She knew but was afraid to be the one to tell him. She looked away.

"The world's a disgrace." His daughter tried her best to keep the anger she felt out of her voice.

"You have to be crazy; it's suicide to go out there now! There are more than four billion others already standing on top of each other. There are a few who are fat and gluttonous, but far more struggling with starvation! The air is foul, the waters aren't fit for consumption, and all the grandeur that used to be has gone up in smoke."

Unable to control himself any longer, Har Megiddo burst into sobs. He wept as though his whole life had been shattered and meaningless.

"Father..." arose a fitful murmur. "Have you no pity? What have you decided must come about?" They entreated him.

"I'll do it," Har Megiddo replied with some great effort. "I'll go out of the valley and see for myself."

"You can't!" Rebecca's hand flew to her mouth. "You're not well enough to undertake so strenuous a journey."

"Enough...!" I have decided that it must come about!"

The north wind roared in, tore the almond tree up by the roots, lifted the house up in the air, then let it go, crashing to the earth. Wave after wave of his children fell down on the cliffs below; thousands of beady white eyes stared up at him through the darkness, watched as he melted away. There remained of him nothing but a hide of flesh wrapped around his spirit to keep it warm as the wind bore it away.

Out of the Valley of the Shadow of Death. The gospel of Har Megiddo spread over the land.

"You're dead! Not alive!"

"You're in hell! Not in Heaven!"

"You're paying for the sins you've committed in life!"

"So, say I, for I am thy Lord, they Creator."

HAR MEGIDDO

www.ingramcontent.com/pod-product-compliance
Lightning Source LLC
Chambersburg PA
CBHW072057170626
46813CB00004B/1393